HORSES *of the* DAWN

WILD BLOOD

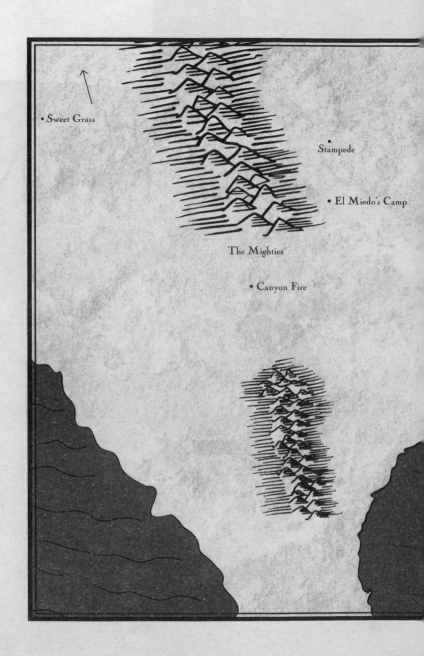

Sweet Grass

Stampede

El Miedo's Camp

The Mighties

Canyon Fire

First
Island

HORSES *of the* DAWN

WILD BLOOD

KATHRYN LASKY

SCHOLASTIC INC.

Copyright © 2016 by Kathryn Lasky

This book was originally published in hardcover by Scholastic Press in 2016.

All rights reserved. Published by Scholastic Inc., *Publishers since 1920*. SCHOLASTIC and associated logos are trademarks and/or registered trademarks of Scholastic Inc.

The publisher does not have any control over and does not assume any responsibility for author or third-party websites or their content.

No part of this publication may be reproduced, stored in a retrieval system, or transmitted in any form or by any means, electronic, mechanical, photocopying, recording, or otherwise, without written permission of the publisher. For information regarding permission, write to Scholastic Inc., Attention: Permissions Department, 557 Broadway, New York, NY 10012.

This book is a work of fiction. Names, characters, places, and incidents are either the product of the author's imagination or are used fictitiously, and any resemblance to actual persons, living or dead, business establishments, events, or locales is entirely coincidental.

ISBN 978-0-545-68301-2

10 9 8 7 6 5 4 3 2   17 18 19 20

Printed in the U.S.A.   40

First printing 2016

Book design by Ellen Duda
Illustrations by Richard Cowdrey

Freedom is not something that anybody can be given.
Freedom is something people take, and people are as free as
they want to be.

—James Baldwin

PART 1

First Lodge

CHAPTER 1

Long Shadows

Joy swept through Estrella as she and Tijo galloped out of the Burnt River Clan's camp. But not just her own joy. The filly also felt the thrill of Tijo's triumph at confronting the healer, the man who'd driven the boy away from his clan. The power-hungry leader had cowered at the sight of Tijo, who'd appeared like something out of a dream, or perhaps a nightmare, wearing a coyote pelt and riding a four-legged creature the healer had never seen before.

But even that couldn't compare to the elation Estrella felt when she realized she'd caught the scent of the sweet grass once more. As long as she could lead her herd to the sweet grass, they would survive in this new world that had become their home.

As she sprinted across the windswept plain with Tijo on her back, Estrella heard the pounding hooves of the herd. She knew the distinct sound of each of the nine horses and the one mule galloping behind her, and let out a joyful whinny as she sensed a fresh spirit take over the old stallion Hold On. She turned her eyes toward him. Although almost blind, Hold On's hooves struck the ground with a new assurance. *The farther we are from humans*, Estrella thought, *the more powerful we become.* The band of low red mountains to the west became a blur. She tossed her head and saw clouds streaking above. Estrella lengthened her stride and stretched out her neck, feeling Tijo automatically lean forward as well. *I shall race the clouds!*

Tijo marveled at the old stallion keeping pace next to them. When Tijo met Hold On, the stallion had been blinded in a canyon fire. His vision had improved slightly, but to this horse, the world was still mostly a shadowy one. While Hold On might not have been able to see the red blur of the mountains or the racing clouds, he could see the slashing shadows cast by the galloping horses around him. In his near blindness, the stallion had become a sifter of shadows, reading the gradations of darkness to light with a deep sensitivity. At the same time, his other senses had been honed to the sharpness of a bone knife's edge.

"You smell the sweet grass?" Hold On asked as he drew up next to Estrella. Although they'd been galloping for some time, he sounded hardly winded.

4

"Yes," she said, though *smell* barely began to describe the sensation. It was as if the grass were streaming through her veins. She could almost taste it. With each stride, she felt the heady mixture of ecstasy and relief. She thrust out her powerful legs and gobbled the land, streaking across the plain like the shooting star for which she had been named.

Sky tossed his head back and whinnied shrilly, "Race!" His playful challenge peeled into the air and electrified the horses. Sky and Verdad bolted across the hard ground and were soon leading, but it didn't take long for Estrella to catch up.

"Race to where?" Arriero asked, pulling up next to her. The heavy stallion caught Estrella's look of surprise and snorted. "What? You think an old stallion can't run fast?"

"I won!" Sky whinnied triumphantly as he skidded to a halt by a large boulder. His odd eyes, one blue and one almost black, glittered.

"You didn't win," Verdad protested. The creamy-white colt was dancing impatiently. In contrast to the rest of his coat, his legs were black from his fetlocks to his hocks. "You just declared the finish line. You can't just make up the rules of a race like that."

"Why not?" Sky said with a snort.

"Not in the middle of a race."

Yazz the mule trotted up to them.

"My goodness!" Corazón exclaimed. The old mare, who had also just arrived, turned to look at Yazz. "Look who's here!"

"Don't be so surprised. I've gained quite a bit of speed since joining the herd. It's amazing how much faster one can go when not in a jerkline pulling a load of rocks." Yazz shook herself vigorously, as if the ghost of a yoke still hovered on her shoulders.

As Estella glanced over at Yazz, she thought how far the mule had come. She'd escaped the most dangerous of enemies — El Miedo, the Iber who was as hungry for horses as he was for gold. Yazz had been a pack mule for El Miedo until, after witnessing one brutal beating too many, she kicked down a fence and bolted, eventually joining up with the first herd.

Early on, Yazz had warned them that this treacherous and violent Iber had his sights set on the first herd. She'd been right. Not long after, the Iber chased the horses to the very edge of a ravine, and Estrella had jumped a nearly impossible distance to clear it. She could remember vividly hanging in midair over the deep chasm, thinking that she would prefer to fall to her death and break into countless pieces than be captured again. And she knew that every single horse of the first herd felt the same as they leapt after her. Better to die free than live in captivity.

The horses stood breathing hard now at the boulder, the so-called finish line. They peeled back their lips and inhaled the pungent scent that swirled around them.

"It's the sweet grass," Estrella whispered reverentially, as if she were afraid it would disappear if she uttered the words too loudly. She scanned the surrounding terrain. It was all hard dirt, without a blade of grass . . . yet never had the scent been so strong. How could they smell it and still not see any grass at all? This was worrisome. They needed good grazing to fatten up and preserve their strength before they attempted to cross the Mighties — Tijo's word for the vast mountain range. Summer was not endless, and winter would come again soon.

But how far behind them were the Ibers? They could ride fast, and with their long lassos that spun out into the air like snakes, they could bring horses at a full gallop down to the ground.

Long before that ravine, El Miedo had captured one horse, Pego the dark stallion, in just this way. But Pego did not seem to mind, and soon became a favorite of El Miedo. It was Pego who had betrayed the first herd by leading the tyrannical Iber to their track.

Pego and El Miedo had made a dangerous team. The two creatures, one horse and one human, were evil entwined and loomed like some monstrous apparition. However, they were not a specter, but very real. Mounted on Pego, El Miedo had run them to the very edge of that ravine. He'd never expected the horses to jump. But they had. At the crucial moment, each member of the first herd had glimpsed something sparkling in the night — the tiny horse that periodically appeared to

Estrella, helping her lead her herd to the sweet grass on the other side of the Mighties. And so they'd leapt, leaving El Miedo and his men gaping in wonder.

However, there were other obstacles ahead. There was no grass in this region. The plants were thorny and tough as wood. Horses were supposed to get fat for winter. Even Tijo, who did not graze but ate meat, found the hunting poor. He had grown thinner before Estrella's eyes, and when he'd mounted Hold On the other day, the stallion had said, "You're so light, I wonder if you're even on my back."

A stream meandered not far away, and Estrella could see Tijo taking out his fishing tackle — the bone hooks he had fashioned, the fishing line he had made from the gut of an animal, and the slender alder limb that he would attach to the hook and line. She admired the orderliness of his quest for food. If he were successful, he would be able to eat. But the herd needed grass, not fish, and there was very little orderliness involved with their own quest for nourishment.

For Tijo was not the only one who had grown thin. The coat of the big, bulky stallion Arriero seemed to hang on him, too large for the gaunt figure inside it. Verdad and Sky, the colts, seemed to swim in their pelts as well. The hip bones of the two mares Angela and Corazón stuck out sharply. Estrella could count their ribs. They were all too skinny for the end of summer. *And so am I*, Estrella thought. But it was the big stallions whose thinness was most visible.

Bella, a mare, had always been thin to begin with; now she seemed frail. She stood under the shadows of a cottonwood tree while the fluffy tufts shed from the branches blew around her hooves. The shiny leaves shimmered and trembled in a light wind as Bella walked up to Estrella.

"What troubles you, Estrella?"

"Look at the stallions. They seem so small, so slight to me."

"Maybe it's because you've grown bigger? You're a filly about to become a mare."

"It's not that. We are all too thin."

"Try not to worry, Estrella. We'll find the sweet grass. You haven't let us down yet. Have faith, young'un. We all have faith in you."

Estrella felt something stir inside her. Did she deserve their faith? Faith was a heavy burden to carry. Heavier than any human who might threaten to capture and ride her with a bit, bridle, and saddle.

Estrella looked toward the range of mountains ahead. She'd always sensed that they would have to cross those mountains to get to the sweet grass. And now she knew for sure. In the twilight, they loomed immense and impassable. The peaks appeared to scrape the moon.

"You know, Bella, Tijo calls those mountains the Mighties."

"It's a good name," Bella said softly. The mare had always spoken quietly, but there'd been an extra tinge of wistfulness in her voice ever since she'd lost her colt.

"We have to get there, but it'll take many days to even reach the foothills."

Bella pricked her ears and looked across the wide, flat plain. "How long do you think?"

"Through the rest of spring and most of summer. We need to cross them by autumn or else the snow will make it impossible." She paused. "And we need to grow fat on good grass before we begin."

The scent of sweet grass might stir through the air, but there was no visible sign of it. Nor could she see the sparkling little horse that appeared in the past like a twinkling constellation, a glimmer on the far edge of the night just before the dawn. Since the first time Estrella caught sight of the little horse, she knew it connected her to a wisdom that stretched through the ages. But now she felt as if she were in a kind of free fall.

The herd thought of her as their leader, but in truth, Estrella was just a follower, being led by the tiny horse on a quest not merely for the sweet grass, but a quest to relive the story of their very origins. They were traveling to the most distant borders of time — a time before time. This land that the Ibers called the New World was not new for the horses. They were coming home.

Bella stepped closer and ran her muzzle through Estrella's tangled mane. "We'll find grass, Estrella. We'll grow fat again.

You'll lead us to the Mighties, and we'll cross them. I have faith. We all have faith."

If they made it, Estrella knew they'd be truly free. There'd be no chance of El Miedo, or any man, forcing them into servitude again.

CHAPTER 2

A Father's Bones

Little Coyote crouched in the shadows, watching the herd. He'd been following the horses since they left the camp of the Burnt River People. Tijo's people had not recognized the boy and had backed away, cowering at what he wore on his head — the head of Little Coyote's father. Never before had they seen a horse. Together, the head, the boy, and the horse fused into one terrifying monster.

It was a gruesome sight for Little Coyote, even though he had never felt anything close to love for his father. In fact, he had loathed him. But this . . . this was terrifying. His father seemed even more horrific in death than he had in life.

Watching Tijo ride away, wearing his father's pelt, Little Coyote had felt an odd mixture of disgust and relief. He was relieved that his cruel father was gone. But then there'd been that head. Where the eyes had been were two terrifying dark holes that peered straight at him, demanding vengeance. If Little Coyote did nothing to avenge his death, would he be haunted by his father until the end of his own life?

Little Coyote had only the briefest memories of his mother. She had died shortly after he had been weaned. Of his father he had too many memories — all of them bad. His body was scarred from the hundreds of bites he had endured from his father's fangs. There were unsightly patches on his rump and shoulders where fur never grew anymore. Little Coyote was a ragtag creature if there ever was one.

But that didn't matter. He was his own creature. He was not a "trickster," although that was the human name for his kind. His father had proudly used the coyote word *apuk*, which covered it all — deceit, tricks, schemes, ruses. "This is our heritage," he would proclaim while swaggering about. But Little Coyote knew that it would never be *his* heritage. "What's wrong with you, boy?" his father would ask repeatedly. He held his son in such utter contempt that he had never even named him. He called him *boy*, which was a clan word, and not *pup*. To call an animal by a human word was the worst insult that a father coyote could confer on a young one. So this nameless pup called himself simply Little Coyote, and as such, he had to endure his father's boastful strutting every time he had pulled some trick. That horrible shrill chant as he pranced around still rang in Little Coyote's ears.

I am coyote,

I am coyote.

I slip and slink

Into your head

So you can't think.

I am the dream stealer,

The fantastic concealer.

Crafty and sly,

I'll sell you lies.

A merchant of death,

I'll swipe your breath.

I am coyote,

I am coyote.

Little Coyote's world had become pleasantly quiet when his father's final trick ended in death during the last of the winter moons. Big Coyote had attacked two horses, the old stallion and the young filly with the star on her forehead. For a short time, the old horse and the coyote wrestled in a tangle on the ground as the boy tried to get a clear shot at Big Coyote with his dagger. Suddenly, a white-faced owl plunged from the sky and snatched Big Coyote in his talons. It flew high into the star-spiked night, and then the owl dropped Big Coyote.

Downwind of the horses, Little Coyote had watched it all, transfixed in horror and amazement. His father, the bragging trickster, was dead, killed by an owl.

Numb with shock and unsure what to do next, Little Coyote had begun following these strange, fascinating creatures who'd defeated his father without tricks, showing great courage.

I should make them pay, he thought. *They are responsible for my father's death, and I shall be haunted forever by him.*

Little Coyote would never forget the moment when he saw his father's skin stretched on the rack of alder branches. After witnessing his father's terrible fall, he'd been careful to stay downwind of the horses. But that night, there was a wind shift and an unexpected yet familiar scent came to him, cutting through every other smell in the high, dry country. As soon as he caught the first whiff, he knew what it was. *His father's bones.*

Little Coyote was perplexed. He'd assumed the scavengers would devour his father's remains. It had also snowed heavily that same evening. So how could he be catching his scent now? A chill ran through him. Had he been right? Would his father's ghost haunt him until he had avenged his death?

He shook his body as if to rid himself of the scent, the wraith of this father. Then he crept as close as he dared, blessing the wind that both blew away any trace of his own scent and carried that of his father's bones. He saw that the bones were stacked neatly in a pile — a disturbing sight, but nothing that would haunt him. But that wasn't all. Little Coyote turned and saw his father's pelt stretched on a rack made from slender branches. He stared in horror. He had seen the clan people do this to hides of sheep or goats, but never with a coyote, for they deemed it ill luck. A sudden wave of dread washed over him. Although he had no love for his father, now he'd need to avenge him so his father's spirit could find his way to the spirit camps.

A moment later, he set off after the horses, following them as quietly as a shadow.

CHAPTER 3

Dangerous Allies

Inside the tent, El Miedo was not praying. He was brooding and cursing. Over and over, he relived the awful scene at the ravine. He had been so close to capturing the herd led by the filly with the star on her forehead, the beautiful filly who'd begun to haunt his dreams. What an animal she was! And then there was the stallion Arriero. A veritable bull of a horse. He was muscular but had great speed.

Who could have imagined that the herd would have jumped that ravine? Something had inspired them. It was almost as if they had been possessed by magic. Had they grown some sort of invisible wings? For indeed they appeared to almost fly.

El Miedo would have followed. He would have jumped. "¡Adelante! ¡Adelante! El Noble. ¡Mi Pego!" The sound of his own voice came back to him as he recalled urging the dark stallion on. The spurs hanging from the tent post were still stained with the blood of the cowardly horse. The stallion had skidded to a dead halt, trembling with fear. The beast named for the winged horse constellation had actually balked! The chase had ended. And then, to add insult to this injury, the stupid animal reared and threw him.

It was utterly humiliating. El Miedo had glimpsed the hint of mirth in his officers' eyes, the bitter glint of misbegotten joy and contempt. Yes, contempt! And he, El Miedo, leader of the largest expedition to cross the sea to this new land, had to be hauled back to camp in a cart pulled by a mule. His twisted back had eventually healed. But there was a deeper wound inside that seemed to fester and feed on his humiliation.

Mules were supposed to be hauling rocks veined with gold and silver. Not *him*. It crushed his pride to have his men witness such indignity. But it wasn't just his fall from Pego. El Miedo had arrived with 600 men, 85 carts, 24 wagons, and over 1,000 animals — horse, mules, burros, and donkeys. His expedition had made his rival the Seeker's look like a bedraggled peasant parade during Holy Week in some dusty village.

But now El Miedo's herd of animals had been halved. First, a treacherous mule, Yazz, had escaped from the corral. Then others began to flee. Who would have imagined that a mule could turn so duplicitous, so faithless? Hadn't he fed the creatures the best grains, for they needed their strength to haul the rocks? So what if his men beat the creatures bloody when they balked? Was it a crime to beat a mule? People had beaten the stupid beasts for centuries. El Miedo's men had been feeding them, hauling water to their troughs all these months. What kind of thanks was that? Discipline was important. And when discipline was breeched, disorder ensued. Over the days following Yazz's escape, other animals found ways to escape as well. Even several of the chickens had somehow sneaked from their coops. In a complete rage, El Miedo ordered fifty of the remaining chickens slaughtered. Which was foolish on his part: Now there were no eggs and the meat had spoiled quickly.

He peeked out from a slit in his tent to regard the animals in the corral. There were simply not enough. Not for his plans. And there was no denying that the beasts had grown thinner, for the grazing was not good and the grain they had brought was growing scarce. But instead of pity, he felt only contempt for the creatures. The mules were growing more stubborn, and the horses had begun balking. They had all seen Pego's treachery. El Miedo felt their scorn, their disdain — their mockery. And he loathed them for it. But he still needed them. He couldn't conquer this land without beasts to carry his supplies and his men.

And where was Coyote? Had the old *perro zorro*, the dog

fox, abandoned him or betrayed him? The creature had twined through his dreams and brought him his first vision of the dark stallion, Pego. He'd taken it as a sign of God and had put his trust and faith in the horse . . .

His competition with the Seeker, who had come a few months before him, was not going as planned. Whoever found gold first, whoever established dominion first in this new land would rule it, become a king. El Miedo ground his teeth. The dream could be restored if he could recapture Pego and the rest of that herd, including the mule. If it was the last thing he did, he'd get that mule back. Then, and only then, could he have his kingdom.

The trail that had dwindled for El Miedo had not for Pego. Picking his way beneath a stony ridge that followed a dry river-bed, he found a clump of good grazing. It was a reddish grass and tastier than a lot of the tough grasses that grew in this dry country. It felt good in his gut. There wasn't much, just a few patches of it here and there, making him glad he's struck out on his own. The grass would never suffice for the ten horses and the mule that made up the first herd. Of this he was glad. The entire herd infuriated him. How he would have loved to seen them captured by El Miedo! He would like to see that cursed filly Estrella bridled and ridden by sharp-spurred Ibers, blood dripping from her flanks.

He knew that the first herd must think him a coward for not leaping the ravine. They had stared back at him with withering disdain as El Miedo had tried to force him to jump. But who were they to judge him? He who'd been named for the winged horse! He would show them all someday.

Unlike his former master, Pego did not lament the disappearance of the *perro zorro*. He sensed that the coyote had betrayed them by leading them to that ravine. Pego tossed his head with a snort. He didn't need that trickster's help. He didn't need anyone.

He could tell that this trail along the ridgeline had been made by the humans the Ibers had called Chitzen. These humans seemed to be moving their village, for there were the signs of drags — animal skins stretched on poles for pulling their worldly goods. There were many clans of Chitzen in this land, none of which had ever seen a horse before El Miedo and the Seeker arrived. Some had thought the creatures were gods! There was a good chance that the humans who'd left this trail still hadn't encountered one. Surely they'd be impressed by an animal as large as himself. Pego inhaled deeply, puffed out his chest, and practiced his *paso fino*, the elegant gait that would make him look regal when he approached. But he was not ready to reveal himself just yet. He needed to find these people and study them before he made his entrance. He'd learned that from Coyote. Although the creature had been a deceitful double-crossing cur, he'd had some clever ideas.

Pego knew what he had to do. He would appear before the human clan like an apparition, and they would revere him like a god! That would show the first herd. That would show the wretched El Miedo! Pego needed no herd. He needed no master. He was destined for greatness on his own.

The night was warm, but the healer of the Burnt River Clan was shivering — shivering under a blanket made from the pelt of the thunder creature. The healer's wife, Pinyot, regarded him with a mixture of contempt and fear. He had sworn her to secrecy. She was not to tell anyone about his condition. After all, he was now not simply the healer but the chieftain of the Burnt River Clan.

He shivered constantly, and his dreams were haunted by terrible visions. He had never recovered from seeing the lame boy Tijo on the enormous, four-legged beast. And with the Trickster's head atop his own! It was a terrible omen. Then, to make matters worse, foolish Pinyot had stupidly opened her mouth about the blanket. She said that perhaps the thunder creature blanket was cursed since it had originally belonged to Haru, Lame Boy's auntie-mother, whom the healer had poisoned. Pinyot had the audacity to suggest that this was all his fault!

But the healer did not feel cursed. He felt diminished and sensed himself shrinking in the eyes of his people, which was worse. Ever since they had seen Lame Boy on that immense animal, towering over the healer, he'd no longer been the most powerful presence in their lives. He knew what he had to do. He must find that huge creature that the lame boy had ridden or one like it. Its spirit might fill him, and if he could ride atop the beast, he would no longer be diminished in the eyes of his people.

He picked up his spear and, without a word to his wife, left the tent.

CHAPTER 4

Long Spirits

Haru knew that though her spirit was strong, the lodge that sheltered it, the *omo* owl, was growing weary. Such was the way with spirit lodges. Although spirits weighed nothing, after a while they leeched the energy of the host. The owl had been a good lodge. Its wings were powerful, its gizzard strong, but it was growing tired. Haru would have to find a new lodge soon.

It was still early morning, but as the sun broke over the land, warm drafts rose, and she lifted effortlessly on the soft billows of air. She marveled as she caught the sound of a mouse's heartbeat as it scampered across the corral. She had grown fond of this lodge and the abilities that it had given her — including the power of flight, allowing her to soar free from earth without stirring a feather. Sounds filtered into her ears, like the heartbeat of that mouse below, and her eyes, on a moonless night, could catch the passage of the blackest wolf through thick grass. A pack of wolves had been stalking El Miedo's animals, and more than once she had torn out of the night and released a terrifying screech that had saved a foal or chicken or one of the goats brought from the Old Land.

But at the moment, Haru had even more pressing concerns than her deteriorating spirit lodge. Somewhere, deep inside, she felt a growing sense of alarm. Something terrible was coming to her Tijo and the horses who had been so good to him. She needed to find them before this lodge wore out. She needed to warn them.

Haru had raised that boy, who'd been abandoned by another clan, and cared for him until she had died. And now he was more horse than boy. Not that it troubled her. She reveled in delight every time she recalled Tijo riding into the Burnt River camp astride Estrella, terrorizing the healer, who had once called Tijo Lame Boy.

But she was growing worried. She had seen El Miedo lusting for the first herd, chasing them to the edge of the ravine. They'd managed to escape him that day. Haru had flown over that ravine and watched as her boy, Tijo, sailed across on the back of the beautiful filly Estrella. For those incredible seconds, they'd all been suspended in the same sky together. But now El Miedo would seek revenge. Haru had seen how he treated animals. She had to do whatever necessary to keep the herd from falling into his clutches.

Haru spread her wings and caught a breeze that took her over El Miedo's encampment. The animals were pathetically thin and worn, their bones jutting out. Two men were trying to shove a small mule into a yoke. The mule was braying and squealing as a man approached with a heavy whip. Was this the destiny of the first herd? To be captured and whipped until the wildness was beaten out of them?

Haru had to seek out Tijo and Estrella and warn them. If only the *omo* owl could make it. The lodge was thinning. She did not have much time and certainly not time to seek a new lodge. Even now, with the billows of warm air easing her flight, her wings were growing weary as she carved a turn to head in the direction she thought the herd had gone. It was almost night by the time she found them, and a full moon was beginning to rise. The air had turned cold. She was exhausted. Her wings felt as if they might simply fall off.

The herd had settled under the spreading branches of a lace tree. It was Angela and Corazón who named the tree, for the delicate leaves reminded them of the mantillas their mistresses had worn in the Old Land. The nearly full moon's silver light filtered down through the leaves, casting cooling shadows in beautiful designs. Unconsciously, the herd had developed a loose arrangement for sleeping. Some stood and some lay down, but the stallions — Grullo, Arriero, Bobtail, and Hold On — were always on the edges of the group. They were equally comfortable standing or lying down. But it was the stallions that would signal the fight or flight command if a predator approached — human, mountain cat, or wolf.

Tonight, they paid particular attention, as wolves had been spotted. Even though they were smaller than horses, wolves could be very dangerous in a large pack. They were cunning killers when working together, and very strategic. Although nearly blind, Hold On was essential to this lookout because of his uncommon powers of smell and hearing.

Tijo was not standing still or lying down. He had walked out from the canopy of lacy light and was scanning the night sky. He saw Hold On's ears twitch, then heard the slither of a rattlesnake some distance off as it coiled to strike prey — most likely a desert rat. The snakes hunted in the cool of the night and slept through the hot days. But the snake posed no danger to the herd. Tijo walked back to Hold On, touched his ears, and whispered, "It's far from here. Go back to sleep, old fellow."

Tijo tipped his head up again. The moon burned silver, and against its bright disk, a pair of wings were printed. "The *omo* owl," he whispered into the starry night as the bird began a steep banking turn. He watched and saw it land in the lower branches of a nearby cedar tree. Its white face glowed like a smaller moon come down to earth. It twisted its head in that odd way of owls, then tipped it to one side to stare straight at Tijo. Then another little twist, followed by a nod toward Estrella, who slept just inside the circle of stallions. There was no mistaking. Both he and Estrella were being summoned.

So Tijo made his way toward the filly. She stood in the customary sleeping position with her forelegs locked. But he could tell she was not asleep. Her withers flinched, a definite sign that she was anxious. Her eyes opened as he stepped toward her.

"Come," he whispered, nodding toward a cedar tree.

"Is it the tiny horse?" Estrella asked, her eyes bright with anticipation.

"No. It's her. She wants to speak with us," Tijo replied. Estrella knew immediately who he was talking about. It was the *omo* owl, the spirit lodge for Haru. The owl sometimes appeared as a male and sometimes as a female. Such was the way of spirits when they lodged within another creature.

The white-faced owl perched on a low branch of the cedar tree. She fixed them both with her large black eyes, then let out a deep sigh as if the spirit of the Haru inside the lodge were profoundly weary.

"Something bad is coming . . ."

"What kind of bad?" Estrella asked, suddenly alert. She jerked her head from side to side, sifting the wind for the scent of a predator.

The owl shook her head. "You are safe at the moment, but not for long."

"What is it?" Tijo pressed.

"My spirit wears thin in this lodge. It is hard for me to see everything. Just take heed. El Miedo needs horses. He is growing desperate and is coming after you. The only way to escape him is to split the herd. That way, he won't be able to lure all of you into a trap."

"Split the herd," Estrella repeated, shocked. The idea went against everything she had worked toward since they had first swum to shore. Apart, the herd was nothing. Together, they had power. What Haru was suggesting was impossible. They had gone through so much to be together. Sacrificed so much. There was the canyon fire that had blinded Hold On. They had escaped together from the City of the Gods. They had confronted mountain cats.

"I know what you are thinking," Haru said, breaking the silence.

"You couldn't possibly know, Haru." Estrella tossed her head and stomped her hoof. "You've never had a herd. Owls travel alone. And even when you were a human, you lived apart from your clan."

"It's going to be okay," Tijo said. He reached up and stroked Estrella's neck, trying to calm her. "Just listen to Haru."

"You must take the long way to the sweet grass." Haru's feathers drooped as she perched on a branch, and although she spoke calmly, there was a note of weary frustration.

"What long way?" Estrella asked. "We're heading toward the Mighties."

"Ahead is the plain of the thunder creatures. If you go across that plain, the Iber will see you clearly and ambush you." She sighed as if trying to summon the strength to say what she had to next. "You must go around the plain to the Mighties."

"But there isn't time. We must get to those foothills by autumn at the latest. If winter comes . . ."

"If you don't heed my warning, you won't see another winter."

Tijo and Estrella exchanged a worried glance. "But if we take the long way, we might not make it across the Mighties before winter comes," Tijo said. "It's too much of a risk."

"Don't argue with me." It was the same scolding tone she had sometimes used with Tijo when he was a small child, but her voice was much weaker. "I feel something bad coming. It whistles down these hollow bones of mine like a cold bitter wind. You must split into two groups and take two different paths around the plains before meeting on the other side of the mountains. It's the only way."

"Are you sure?" Tijo's voice trembled.

"Am I sure?" The *omo* owl seemed to bristle and appeared twice her size. Then she immediately shrank again and seemed smaller than ever. "Tijo, when have I ever not done what I think is best for you? Yes, I am sure."

"Don't be angry, Auntie."

"I am not angry. I am weak. The spirit camps are calling me back. My lodge frays." The black eyes of the *omo* owl pierced through him. She opened her sharp beak wide and inhaled deeply, then spread her wings and staggered into flight.

Little Coyote had been listening from a burrow he had dug downwind of the first herd. He was surprised now to catch the sound of the owl's wings just outside. Then the owl peeked in, its luminous white face filling the opening, and he nearly yelped in astonishment . . .

"You're not afraid of me?" Little Coyote asked.

"Why should I be afraid of you?"

"Every creature is. They think we are . . . are . . ."

"Tricksters?" the *omo* owl asked.

"Well . . . er . . . yes. Deceitful. Dishonest."

The *omo* owl cut him off. "I think you are worthy of trust. But I am weak, so I must speak fast."

Little Coyote was stunned. "You mean you don't think I am like my father?"

"Not in the least. I trust you."

"Why?"

"I am a spirit. Spirits see long. But as I said, I am very tired for reasons you won't understand, not now — perhaps later."

Little Coyote cocked his head slightly. In the vaporous mist above the crown of the owl's head, he saw a twinkling. "What . . . what's that?"

"A small horse? The tiny horse? Is that what you see?" The owl's voice was low but urgent. Little Coyote nodded. "That's the proof," the owl continued with a hint of satisfaction.

"The proof of what?"

"That you are worthy of trust. It means you might be called upon."

"Called upon to do *what?*" Little Coyote had one task: to avenge his father's murder. The last thing he needed was to talk nonsense with this strange creature.

"To help the horses and the boy who rides with them. The first herd."

"Help them? How can I help them? They killed my father. It makes no sense."

But before he could ask the *omo* owl another question, the sparkling tiny horse dissolved into the mist. The owl had not even spread her wings. She just vanished without a sound.

Wait and they will come, Pego thought to himself. He had been following the Burnt River Clan for a few days. Their leader was immediately identifiable for the peculiar kind of "crown" that he wore. It was unlike any of the gold, jewel-studded royal crowns he'd seen in the Old Land. From the center of this "crown" the antlers of a deer soared, and from its branches hung the curved fangs of a mountain cat. The chieftain carried a club that was similarly festooned with the claws and teeth of ferocious animals. Striding beside him was a large brutal dog. He had all the accoutrements of power, and yet Pego smelled weakness, fear, and vanity. *Perfect!* thought Pego. *He is ready to meet his god! And I am that god!*

For the next day and a half, Pego laid down meticulous clues, not only his hoofprints, but his waste. The dog was quick to find every clue. But Pego played it cleverly, continuing to elude the chieftain and the dog until he felt the time was exactly right. He had to admit to himself that he had learned a great deal from the traitorous coyote. Hadn't the creature made him wait until the time was perfect to reveal himself to El Miedo? So now he waited for the ideal night, a flawless night when the moon was a quarter, not half, and when his constellation, Pegasus, was rising in the eastern sky. There could be no mist, not a drop of vapor to dull the starlight. His dark coat, nearly as black as the sky, would catch the reflection of those heavenly bodies, from the sceptered moon to the starry constellations.

This perfect night had finally arrived. From his vantage point concealed by a thick stand of scrub, he could hear the dog's panting and the footfalls of his master, the chieftain. There was no wind, and as the chieftain drew closer, Pego caught the small clacking sounds of the fangs and claws that jiggled from his headdress and club. Cloaked in symbols of power, this fool human thrust through the night.

Pego watched the transit of the moon. He wanted it to be directly over his own head, to hover like a celestial crown. He waited patiently, his heart pounding in his chest. A few more heartbeats. One . . . two . . . three . . . four . . . He erupted from the scrub and, with his magnificently arched back, reared and pawed at the sky. He felt the rush of the *Pura Raza* blood in his veins, the bloodlines of the Jennets, the Barbs, the most noble horses to gallop across the earth. God's horses.

It worked precisely as Pego had thought. The chieftain was overwhelmed and so was the dog. They fell to their knees, trembling in awe and fear. Pego reared two, three times. Then began to buck. The ground shook. The chieftain and his dog cowered, but they were transfixed and could not scrape their eyes from this spectacle. Then it all stopped. Stopped as suddenly as it began. The horse, glistening in sweat, stood perfectly still. The chieftain dared not breathe. What happened next was perhaps the most miraculous moment of all. This mighty creature began to walk slowly, almost docilely toward him and his dog. He halted a short distance away, and slowly but effort-lessly, considering his size, Pego lowered himself onto his knees in a gesture of complete submission and obeisance. The reflec-tions of the stars still gleamed on his dark coat. It was as if a piece of the heavens had been torn from the night; it was as if a celestial god had descended to pay homage to an earthly god.

Pego was surprised, but the chieftain sat well astride him. He had fashioned a crude halter from rope and with a bit made of bone was able to guide Pego to where he wanted to go. He had no saddle, of course, but had slung a blanket over his back. He had no spurs, either. But such tackle and tools were unnec-essary. Pego and the chieftain had an understanding. But they were not equals. That was important. The chieftain thought that Pego was truly a god and that the horse could give him power, the power he needed not just to lead as a chieftain but to dominate the people of the Burnt River Clan and the clans beyond. The clans of the Blue Deer People, the Bone River People, the Walking Bear People, and the People of the Salt. All these he could control — a territory so vast that it would reach to the edges of where the Mighties grew from the earth and where the legend said more gods dwelled.

His people, those of the Burnt River, were impressed. His mate had become even more docile and without his prompting began making her corn mush stew for the horse. Now, as Pego carried the chieftain through the encampment, the people parted. They were trembling, and their eyes were wide with fear and reverence. *Respect,* thought the chieftain. *Veneración,* thought Pego in the language of the Old Land. "Commander," whispered the chieftain. *Dios,* Pego neighed softly. *Tyrant and devil,* thought the chieftain's mate, Pinyot. The woman was trembling so much that the pan of grain she had just roasted nearly spilled from her hands. The dark stallion liked this. Her fear, the people's fear, was as nourishing as the grain the woman carried. He knew his old master, El Miedo, dreamed of gold and dominion, dreamed of becoming a king in this new world. But he, Pego, could become a god — and kings served gods. And lest that stupid man had forgotten, gods could, with one buck, throw kings from their backs.

CHAPTER 5

Little Coyote's Dream

Little Coyote woke up with a start, the strange encounter with the owl still weighing heavy on his mind. "I have a mission. I am to be called upon. But called upon for *what?*"

The owl had said he had a mission to complete. But surely she couldn't have meant it. *How can I help them when I seek vengeance for killing my father? And even if I knew how to help, they would never trust me. The boy wears the pelt of my father on his shoulders, with my father's head atop his own head. Does he need another coyote pelt to keep him warm? Another head?*

"Called upon?" He murmured to himself. "Called upon to help the horses?"

All through the next day and into the night and then another day, Little Coyote shadowed the first herd. Initially, he tracked them as he would any enemy, but soon he came to know them as well as he had ever known any creatures.

The filly Estrella was anxious. He could tell. Even in her sleep, she muttered to herself. Despite the fact that Little Coyote had never exchanged a word with her, he felt her anguish. He also listened to the natterings of the two old mares, who did not seem anxious like the filly. He could tell that these two were very kind and gentle.

You can't think like that, he reminded himself. *The hide of your father is worn by the boy Tijo.* And Little Coyote's honor depended on avenging his father. He would have to kill one of them, exact a price. But which one should pay? The boy who wore his father's head? That would be justice — wouldn't it?

The boy was closer to Little Coyote's size than the rest of the herd, but he was quick and alert. The colts, Verdad and Sky, were curious but easily distracted. Little Coyote, who had been watching them from behind a dense thicket of sagebrush since the sun had set, shifted his position. He could tell the wind was about to change. The remarkable blind stallion could tell, too. He seemed to know things before they happened. Little Coyote lived in fear that the old fellow they called Hold On would discover him. He knew that these creatures would revile him if they ever caught his scent, for he dragged with him a horrible history. The history of his father's betrayals of the first herd.

And yet Little Coyote was inexorably drawn to them —
to the daring and fearless filly, the wise old stallion Hold On,
the steady mule Yazz. All of them, from the two elderly mares,
Corazón and Angela; to the bold stallions, Grullo, Arriero,
and Bobtail; and the young colts, Verdad and Sky. Although
they shared not one drop of blood, this herd was a family.
Little Coyote had never been part of anything despite the
blood he had shared with his father, and now he was torn.
Part of him wanted nothing more than to be part of such a
family. And part of him knew he was honor-bound to tear it
apart.

Scouts had been dispatched, for there were signs that the first
herd was near. Some of the men rode horses; others were on
mules. Jacinto sniffed the air, pricking his large ears back and
forth, ignoring the man who sat clumsily upon his back.

Jacinto had already decided that if indeed he did find the
track of the first herd, the one that his old friend Yazz had
joined, he would do nothing to betray it to the lowly scout
who now rode him. Yazz, that wise old she-mule, had been his
friend, and how he cursed himself for not having the courage to leave the night Yazz had escaped. But things had not
yet gotten so bad then in El Miedo's expedition. And Jacinto
himself had been a different mule — a good and obedient

mule in the jerkline. However, El Miedo had begun growing more desperate by the day for gold, for more horses, for power. Never a kind man, he had become extraordinarily cruel, particularly when he heard that his archrival, the Seeker, had discovered gold to the south and captured Chitzen to use as slaves.

Suddenly, more was demanded of the animals. Young mules hardly two months old were put in the yoke and beaten savagely if they did not pull the carts meant for mules twice their size. Some of the prize *Pura Raza* horses were even put in harnesses for hauling. This was unheard of in the Old Land. It was not only an affront to the noble bloodlines of the Barbs and Jennets, but they were ill suited to the task. Such horses were good in battle, disciplined and quick, with a powerful grace. But could they pull a fully loaded cart? Not really. None of them had the sure-footedness of an ordinary draft horse or a mule. Therefore they, too, were beaten, beaten until their haunches were bloody. The abuse had increased as the number of horses and mules had decreased.

Jacinto in turn grew more and more ornery, and his back became striped with the marks of the whip. But the mule was not simply stubborn; he had begun to draw other animals to him in the corral and spread the story of Yazz's inspiring escape. El Miedo grew suspicious of Jacinto. Although the man did not understand the brayings, he sensed that the mule was fast becoming a leader of sorts and finally confined Jacinto to a stall. Nonetheless, his old friends came to visit him. Through the cracks, they would whisper in low brays. Abelinda was especially attentive. They had long talks about Yazz's escape and why neither one of them had left that night.

It was odd how the cruelty had then begun to spread. The young boy who hauled water buckets to the troughs had always been, if a little dull, still nice enough. But after he saw a sergeant beating on a *Pura Raza*, he thought nothing of kicking a mule in the side of his head for refusing to get in the yoke. This instinct for brutality was like a contagious disease. Instead of valuing the animals that remained, the men became infuriated with them. And those who weren't the perpetrators of cruelty simply ignored it. The padre who gave the blessings for the animals on Saint Francis Day turned his head the other way when he saw an animal being beaten, as did the blacksmith who took such care when hammering the shoes on a horse. It struck Jacinto that evil was always greater than the sum of its parts. Some men looked away and did not see it, others picked up a whip and joined in, but all in their own way were evildoers. Evil did not just happen. It had to be agreed upon and, oftentimes, silently.

Yazz was the smartest, bravest mule Jacinto had ever known. Why hadn't he gone with her that night? He could have. Or why not the following nights when others began escaping?

Jacinto had asked himself this a thousand times. He had actually been named by his first owner, a priest, for a saint that performed miracles. *But I can't perform miracles*, he had thought to himself. And he certainly was no saint. Then it dawned on Jacinto that before miracles could happen or be performed, one had to be brave. He wasn't very brave. That was his problem.

Now, carrying a lowly scout, Jacinto made his way down a narrow trail. The man sat clumsily, but heavier than the scout was the weight of the scout's indignation. He was furious that he had been assigned this disreputable beast as his mount. Jacinto felt the scout's rage with each swat of the crop on his haunches. He mumbled incessantly: "I am the son of Don Fernando, the richest man in the province of Castile. I am pure Castilian, a fourth cousin twice removed of the king. Yes, the king, and a sixth cousin just once removed of the Holy Roman Emperor. And yet they give me a mule. A stupid waddle-hipped mule."

You should bless those waddle hips of mine, Jacinto thought. *They got you down that gorge this morning.* A moment later, he caught the trace of a familiar smell. An alarming smell. He stopped in his tracks.

"What is it, you fool mule?" The scout cracked his crop on Jacinto's left haunch, but the mule barely felt it. He snapped his head down toward the smell. There were fragments of a lump of dung, horse dung and a distinctive hoofprint. A horse's hoof shod with the special shoes reserved for an owner's favorite horse. It bore the initials *I. de C.* Ignatio de Cristobal, the owner's Christian name, or better known as El Miedo. Pego! The dark stallion was near.

CHAPTER 6

Grace and Hope

The country stretched before the herd as they walked across a ridgeline that rimmed the vast plains of the thunder creatures. The wind rippling through the tall grasses reminded Estrella of the soft billowing ocean waves she had spied when they had all been cast overboard from the ship. Were there savage creatures in this sea of grass that might kill them, as the great shark had devoured her dam? Should they split now, right now, and go the long way around to get to the Mighties? She looked back at the herd. They were all unbearably thin like herself. They needed to get to the sweet grass as soon as possible. But there was grass out there in front of her. Yes, it was coarse, made for the thunder creatures, but they could eat it. And who knew if they went the long way that there would be good forage at all. It seemed insane not to take what was right in front of them.

Time was not the only problem. If they did arrive in the foothills of these mountains weak and on the brink of winter, what would be their chances of surviving? They needed to go now and cut directly across the plains. Tijo said it would not take more than two nights and a day. They must go! Haru was wrong. She did not understand how much nourishment they needed — she was a spirit after all. She weighed nothing. When she spoke of her lodge of the *omo* owl growing thin, that was the owl — not her.

I know what my calling is . . . but how can I ever do it? Little Coyote felt beleaguered with confusion. He was stuck in a maze of unanswerable questions. Did that crazy *omo* owl really not understand how the horses would treat him? How they must hate him? How could that owl dare even think that Little Coyote's destiny and the herd's were connected in any way but the worst way? His father had deceived the horses. The majestic old stallion, the one called Hold On, had been blinded because Little Coyote's father had led them into that canyon where they had all nearly perished from the fire. If Little Coyote approached, they would think he was like his father and that he was there to trick them again.

But strangest of all was that Little Coyote, who had set out to seek vengeance for his father's death, now felt only empathy for his killers. Still, he did not know how he could summon the courage to act on what he felt. *I am a coward!*

How had all this transpired? How had he set out to destroy and then changed his mind? He felt doomed to a life of complete desolation. Not just doomed but cursed by his kind. His father when he chanted one of his boastful and taunting songs would often call himself First Angry. The words of the song clanged in his head.

I am coyote,
I am coyote.
First Angry they call me.
I am the dream maker
and the dream taker.

But why had his father been so angry? What had made him and all the creatures of their kind so angry? Little Coyote was exhausted from the disturbing thoughts that had his mind in a complete tangle. He combed the ground with one paw the way he often raked his fur when trying to scratch out a burr. He had a dim memory of his mother once running her paws gently through his pelt. Grooming, she called it. But all grooming had stopped when she died. He had become a veritable burr ball until he had learned to groom himself as best he could.

"Stop!" a tiny voice squeaked with alarm. Though the voice was small, it startled Little Coyote. He heard an insistent buzzing and swiveled his head this way and that, trying to find the source.

"Can't you see what you're doing?"

"Doing? I can't even see you."

"I'm right here. Do I have to land on your nose, for pity sake?"

Little Coyote blinked. Then his eyes crossed as a pink blur flew in front of his face.

"Wh . . . wh . . . what is that?"

"A petal."

"A flower petal?"

"Yes. *Calochortus plummerae*, to be exact."

"What?"

"More commonly known as a high desert lily. Now kindly remove your paw from my nest."

"I'm on your nest?"

"Yes, you are about to scratch through. I haven't plugged it completely, as I need a few more petals. So if you will quickly remove your paw, I can give you a peek."

"A peek at what?" Little Coyote pulled back his paw. There indeed was a little hole that had not been made by his claws.

"The chamber!" the bee said in a hushed voice. "The larval chamber."

"Larval?"

"My eggs, the larvae, when the nest is ready."

She buzzed in a descending swirl. There was a tiny spray of dirt. "Watch closely," she called back from the hole. Little Coyote pressed closer.

"Do you see?" the tiny voice called up from the hole.

"It's dark."

"Let your eyes get used to it."

It is always dark for me, Little Coyote thought. But just as he was having this doleful thought, he saw a smear of colors within the dimness. He blinked. There was pink and lavender, a lovely blue and a rich orange just the color of the sun as it set. He gasped.

"Are you seeing anything yet?"

"Yes! Yes! It's like . . . like a rainbow. An underground rainbow!"

"It's a nursery for my little ones. Just think how happy they will be when they hatch out. But first things first. I haven't even laid the eggs yet. One more petal and I'll be ready. Perhaps some antelope brush. The stamens are the prettiest yellow. I think it will go nicely with the orange from the scarlet sage. I would love to have coral bean, lovely color, but the petals are poisonous. Wouldn't want my babies hatching out near them. Be back in a sec."

She buzzed off. Little Coyote was in a state of complete amazement. He felt he had entered some magical realm. He peered down the hole again.

"Move over, dear. Quickly, please. I have a nice moist petal here. Must work quickly. Got to plaster it up. That's how we get things to stick. A recipe handed down from the Great Os."

"Great Os?"

"Our founder, dear. The first bee, Osmina the Divine. We're all mason bees. We build our nests, our larval chambers, with mud. The Chitzen think they discovered it for their dwellings, but we were the first to use mud. We know where to dig." Little Coyote had very keen hearing, and the flutterings of the creature's wings and the little bristly hairs on her legs made for quite a racket. "And let me say this. We work alone. Independent. No colonies for us. No slaves. Worker bees, as some call them — what a euphemism!"

"Euphemism? What's that?"

"A nice way of saying something bad."

Little Coyote cocked his head. He liked this creature. He liked her directness. She was . . . was . . . a word hovered in his mind. She was genteel. He had no idea where that word had come from. But he knew it was the right one.

"What's your name?" Little Coyote asked.

"My name is Grace."

"Oh, it fits you! You make beauty. You know flowers. You turn mud into something lovely. You are magical."

"Not at all, my dear. An artist perhaps, a bit of a botanist and a builder with a knack for masonry. But not a magician." She paused. "And what's your name?"

Little Coyote broke away, lowering his head in embarrassment. "I . . . I . . . I . . . have no name."

"No name!" she said in a shocked voice. Little Coyote shook his head. "That is preposterous. We must find you a name."

We, thought Little Coyote. No one had ever said "we" to him.

"I think . . ." Little Coyote began hesitantly. "I think my mum might have said my name once before she died. I can't remember now. I was just a tiny pup. But I honestly think my mum had hopes for me." Little Coyote said nothing about his father.

"Well then, I shall call you Hope." Grace fluttered her wings and made a happy buzzing sound. There was a shimmering vibration of color that radiated through the air as she placed another petal on the larval chamber.

And Little Coyote, too, seemed to feel a shimmer within. *I have a name! I am Hope! I am not my father. I shall answer my calling!* Although he was unsure what that calling might be, he knew he would answer it when the time came.

Hope glanced at the petal Grace had just stuck on.

"*Calochortus plummerae* — that petal you just stuck on. Right?"

"Oh, my, Hope, you are a quick one."

"It's a fancy name for desert lily, right?"

"Right you are again. You're going to go places, Hope. That you are!"

"Thank you . . . thank you. You have given me so much, Grace. A name to start with, and now that I have a name . . . I can continue on my mission."

"Then get along . . . get along, dear."

"Dear." She called me dear. No one had ever called him dear before. The very word was like a drop of honey.

"I might see you again," Grace said. "When the *Gilia sinuata* bloom. Lovely flower. Bluish. It's as if tiny pieces of the sky have drifted to earth. "

"Yes, yes . . . when the gilia blooms." And Little Coyote bounded off, leaping over a low bush bursting with purple blooms. *Hope, my name is Hope!*

Grace was calling after him. "The bush you just leapt, it's a catchfly — *Silene antirrhina.* Similar to but not to be mistaken for the . . ." But the bee's voice was caught by the wind and carried away in the opposite direction.

CHAPTER 7

Gods and Monsters

Estrella led on with Tijo on her back. After much anguished thought, she'd decided to stick to her original plan and not follow Haru's orders to split the herd. The grass was hardly tasty in the region, but it satisfied their hunger. And there was no denying that they were making good time. The Mighties seemed closer each day.

They were within a day's run of the plains of the thunder creatures. The filly knew that these plains was inextricably linked to Tijo's earliest memories — that of the white blanket he had been swaddled in as an infant, made from the hide of the thunder creature that Haru's mate had brought down.

Haru had described the scene of the hunt — how the massive herd of creatures rolled across the plains like a dark and tumultuous sky. Then, in the midst of this herd, a whiteness suddenly appeared. At first, the hunters thought it was a dust witch. The band was fearful and dropped back in its pursuit. All except Haru's mate, Atah, who fearlessly charged forward and flung his spear. The other hunters gasped as they saw a spurt of dark blood against the blue of the sky. The creature was *not* a spirit, but made of flesh and bone. Atah was also clearly made of flesh and bone, for in the act of bringing down the beast, he had been felled himself and trampled to death. Nevertheless, it was his spear in the hide of the thunder creature, and therefore the hide belonged to his mate, Haru. Such were the rules of the clan.

Tijo's mind was filled with the vivid images of the story Haru had been telling him since he was an infant. Estrella, too, knew the story and felt a thrill at the prospect of seeing these thunderous herds. But it was with a blend of fear and hope, for across the plains the immense mountains known as the Mighties grew larger and more oppressive. Their ragged peaks loomed like the mouth of a beast ready to devour them. Should they have listened to the *omo* owl that sheltered Haru's spirit? Estrella could turn the herd now. They could still go the long way. She glanced at them. Was it possible that despite this coarse grass, they had grown even thinner? Doubts began to swirl in her head.

The herd gathered on a promontory overlooking a shallow basin they had to cross before reaching the plains. A chill wind sprang up and rattled the thin branches of the trees they stood under. The high clouds crawling above began to shred, revealing slashes of blue — blue like a river they had recently crossed. A single bird was framed between the clouds. Estrella tipped her head up and traced its flight. The bird was soaring effortlessly on the drafts of air and moving closer and closer to the highest of those ragged peaks of the Mighties. *If only . . .* Estella thought. *If only to be a bird and soar over the crests.* Then they would be safe. Then they would be beyond the reach of humans, of everything that threatened their existence as the first wild herd in this land. They needed to reach this safe place behind the mountains. This Beyond where the sweet grass grew. Estrella felt a sudden thudding in her veins, a quickening in her mind's eye and on the very edge a glimmering. The tiny horse! This was a sign surely that they were on the right path.

"The animals, Tijo, the ones you call the thunder creatures. They are big, aren't they?" Estrella asked, trying to prepare herself for what lay ahead.

Tijo's eyes widened. "They are huge!"

"How huge?"

"From its withers to the ground, maybe about as tall as you, Estrella."

The filly was perplexed as she tried to imagine an animal that stood as tall as herself but wasn't a horse. "Are they like deer?"

Tijo thought how to explain this. He had only seen a thunder creature's face once, when men of the Burnt River Clan had dragged back the carcass to the camp to butcher. "A thunder creature's face is as long as I stand tall."

"What?" Estrella snorted and laid back her ears. It was freakish and profoundly disturbing to try to even imagine such a creature.

"We have to be careful to stay out of their way. They can be very dangerous when they're frightened."

"They sound like monsters, Tijo."

"We're all monsters to ones who haven't seen us before."

At this same moment, Pego stood under the cooling shade of the brush arbor the chieftain's people had erected for him. They treated him well. Like a monarch. A god. The people of the clan approached him with a trembling deference, as if they did not just respect this peculiar beast, but feared him.

The wind shifted, and a new scent wafted on the warm morning breeze. A familiar scent. Pego whinnied nervously and pawed the ground. El Miedo! The dogs were stirring, as they had picked up the scent as well, and now the people were alerted. For the clan was so attuned to their dogs that the creatures did not even need to bark before the humans began moving out of their shelters, spears in hand. The chieftain strode toward Pego and swung up onto his back. Pego was anxious. He was a god to these Chitzen, but not to the Ibers. Not to El Miedo, who had been betrayed when Pego balked at the ravine, refusing to jump and then tossing the man onto the ground.

The chieftain met El Miedo and his men at the edge of a grassy swale. Pego surveyed the scene and was instantly suspicious. The Iber men did not ride. *Odd*, he thought. The only creature they had brought with them was the mule Jacinto. Pego bared his teeth and whinnied shrilly. The chieftain stroked his shoulder to calm him. *Me . . . need calming?* thought Pego. *Not me. You, my friend, will be the one who needs reassuring. I can throw you off in two seconds and be gone.*

The instant Pego spotted Jacinto with the heavy wooden chest strapped to his back and the two bulging saddlebags, he knew the plan. The game! It had begun. A strand of pearls dripping out of one of the saddlebags confirmed this.

And now the seduction begins. How often had Pego seen this played out before. The Ibers would advance into a village, offering baubles in colors these people had never before seen. Bright twinkling jewels, all worthless glass beads, but still they caught the eye. The fabric, however, had the greatest appeal. There was all manner of richly embroidered cloth, some with designs of flowers or animals. A favorite of the Chitzen to the south showed illustrations from the Bible, and yet these people knew nothing of the Bible, the Virgin Mary, or the saints.

Now, the two groups faced each other and a silent scene began to unfold. It was like a pantomime. Each gesture was greatly exaggerated by El Miedo and his men. The slow opening of the chest. The long strands of glass beads lifted and then spilling like liquid jewels in a shimmering waterfall. There was much bowing and head nodding. The chieftain appeared unmoved, but Pego could feel his knees grip harder and sensed a growing excitement in the man. Suddenly, the stallion felt a pair of eyes fastening on him. Jacinto. He had barely acknowledged the stupid beast, so why was the mule staring at him so hard?

They're doing it . . . Jacinto thought. *Pego knows the Ibers' deceit . . . I know it.* Jacinto had seen this done before. In the beginning, the baubles and bright cloth captured the Chitzen's imagination, and then the Ibers captured their bodies, enslaving them.

Jacinto knew El Miedo was looking for the perfect place to build a city, not just a city but a capital in the New Land. The Iber had not given up on finding gold, but a city in many ways was as valuable as gold. A city could even draw gold to it, as a magnet draws iron filings. If he had a city, he would declare himself the governor general, the first in this territory. And every city needed a road leading to it. *"El Camino . . .*

El Camino . . ." How often had Jacinto heard the captain say those words. This *camino* would not be simply a road, but a highway — El Camino Real to welcome His Majesty, the king, and his queen to the New Land. For that, he needed human workers who would become slaves just like Jacinto.

You fool, Jacinto thought, looking at Pego. *That chieftain you carry will soon be in a harness like me.* And then the words that had haunted him since the night Yazz escaped burst in his mind. *Why didn't I go that night? Why didn't I go!* Because he had been too frightened. He was a coward. *Only the brave deserve miracles.* He felt the scout and a lieutenant remove the heavy chest from his back.

Until this moment, these Chitzen had never seen an Iber. If they saw a gun, they, too, would flee, and El Miedo would lose his future slaves. "*Ya habrá tiempo para las mosquetes y las pistolas. Créame. Ahora es el momento para la fe.*" There will be time for muskets and pistols, but for now, faith.

Faith. Jacinto laughed as he caught the word. *He thinks his future slaves should have faith.* He whinnied and twisted his head, feeling the pressure of the bridle against his face. "Faith for fools." He brayed. "There is no such thing as faith." But a gust of wind had blown up, shredding the sound of his voice, slamming the words back into his own long ears. *What use anyhow?* he thought. The Chitzen did not understand the language of mules or horses or Ibers.

The Chitzen had been born wild. What did they know of Ibers and whips, and these people's strange world of God, virgins, and priests? They would soon wear harnesses and be yoked into human jerklines — beast of the Iber burden and lust for gold.

CHAPTER 8

Beasts of the Plains

Before the first herd saw them, they smelled them. The musky scent of the thunder creatures rolled across the plains.

"Are we halfway there, to the Mighties, do you think?" Verdad asked, trotting in place, unable to contain his excitement.

"Verdad, you've been asking that since the last full moon!" Angela scolded gently.

Estrella wrinkled her nostrils. It was a dark and damp night. Dew hung in the air. Thick clouds roiled across the sky, obliterating the stars. But still she could see the Mighties, and they did seem closer than ever. She was sure she had made the right decision. Had they gone around, there could have been rivers to cross, rivers with strong currents to swim against. The herd was energized now. There was a quickening to their steps. Even the old mares were infused with a new vigor.

"I can't see the Mighties; I can feel them," Hold On snorted. And indeed there were cool drafts that must have blown down from their lofty peaks.

"I remember," Arriero spoke in a soft voice that signaled he was reaching through the past to the time when he was a war horse in the Old Land. "We were in the north, in the Sierra del, oh . . . how did they say it in the Iber tongue — *árboles blancos*, I believe."

"Oh, you mean birch trees, those thin white trees," Corazón said.

"Except nothing was white after the battle. It was all red with blood. We lost many. But the enemy lost more." He snorted. "They might have changed the name to the Sierras del Sangre, the mountains of blood."

A shiver ran through Estrella. Had she made the right decision? Or would these plains turn red with their own blood? She knew that the horses would die before they would let themselves be captured again. She picked up the pace.

Sensing her anxiety, Tijo leaned forward and stroked her neck, then changed the subject. "That smell is the hair of the thunder creatures. It's long and thick, and gives off a strong scent."

"Do you mean their manes?" Hold On asked.

Tijo shook his head. "They don't have manes. Not like you."

"No manes?" Angela tsked in disapproval. "How sad. My dam always said my mane was my crowning glory. How she used to groom it."

"I groom it," Corazón huffed.

"Of course, dear, of course."

"If they don't have manes, what do they have?" Sky asked, shaking his own mane to convey his shock.

"It is as if all their pelt is a mane. It's all long and shaggy. Each strand as long as this!" He pulled an arrow from his quiver.

"By my withers!" Angela exclaimed. "It's amazing they don't trip over themselves with manes that long."

"They never trip," Tijo replied as they continued to canter along in an easy loping gait.

"Remember the Infanta Eleanora , daughter of the Princesa Sofia?" Angela asked. "She had braids down to her ankles, and she used to trip on them all the time."

"Until she died," Corazón offered dryly.

"Died?" Tijo asked. He rarely paid attention to the two old mares' gossip. "From tripping on her braids?"

"Oh, no," Corazón replied. "One got caught in a carriage wheel. *¡Terminado!*" The two old mares could on occasion be rather maudlin about their old days in the royal courts, and would unconsciously lapse into the language of the Ibers.

"Were you pulling the carriage, Angela?" Estrella asked.

"We both were," Corazón replied.

"You don't seem terribly sad," Estrella said, twisting her neck so she could exchange a glance with Tijo.

"Oh, the Infanta Eleanora was a horrid little brat. Ghoulish. She had her servants sharpen her spurs when she would ride us and delighted to see blood run from our flanks."

"What?" Estrella asked, startled. She didn't understand how the mares could speak so casually about such horrors.

"It's true," Corazón said. "Oh, how we celebrated when she died."

"But then came the bad part." Angela's voice had lost its air of amusement, and her eyes had a slightly haunted look.

"The bad part?" Sky asked. The herd had stopped cantering and was now gathered around, listening to the mares' story. "What was the bad part?"

"We were sold," Angela said, closing her eyes, as if to shut out the painful parts of the memory.

"Sold to different owners. We were separated for . . . what was it? Five years?" Corazón continued.

"More like six," Angela said.

Estrella shuddered. She and Hold On had only been separated for a few weeks, and the pain had been nearly unbearable. That's what it was like, being part of a herd. Losing a member was like losing a part of yourself.

"You always exaggerate, Angela. It wasn't six. But it felt like ten. I'll never forget the day that you showed up. I had just weaned my little colt, and they took him right away to sell. I hadn't even named him yet. He was such a beauty. Oh, how I ached for him! I thought my heart had broken, and I'd be alone for the rest of my life. But then suddenly in the pasture I saw a mare with spots on her muzzle coming toward me. I would recognize those spots anywhere. 'Fea!' I whinnied. For, as you all know, Angela had been named Ugly for the spots on her muzzle. But to me, she was not 'Fea' at all but the most beautiful sight in the world. My Fea was back. It was consolation after losing my colt . . ." She trailed off, the memory of the joyful reunion with Angela still marred by the shadow of grief.

The horses fell silent. Perhaps they were all thinking of the many partings they had endured in their lives. Few had had such luck to be reunited with those for whom they cared so deeply. Estrella could never hope to be reunited with Perlina, her dam.

Their thoughts were interrupted. Snorts and windy exhalations laced the air. "The thunder creatures are getting up to move. You'll see them now," Tijo said, looking around excitedly. "There's a wallow over there, probably near some good grazing — thunder grass, the clan calls it."

The wind shifted and the odor of the thunder creatures

became sharper. Estrella signaled that they should start walking, but only at a soft-hoof walk. She swung her head four times in each direction. The meaning was clear — no snorting, no whinnying, no wheezing. Absolute quiet so as not to disturb the huge beasts. Even though the horses could not see them because of the thickening fog, the creatures had to be very close.

They walked in silence. Even the large stallions' hooves made no noise as they struck the ground. The familiar sounds of the horses' breath faded away, as if the animals were more spirit than flesh and blood.

Suddenly, Tijo tensed on Estrella's back. "No," he whispered.

Although there had not been a single sound from the first herd, something had disturbed the creatures. The ground began to shake. As the fog thinned in the distance, that part of the earth was buckling up into a new mountain range, but this one was a mere half league away. The landscape, the very sky-line was changing before their eyes.

"Is that an earthquake?" Bobtail neighed tensely.

"No! Hush!" Tijo said urgently. "These are huge animals. Whenever they move in a herd like that, you will feel something beneath your hooves."

"What is that dark dust cloud? Darker than the night?" Estrella asked.

"That's the thunder creatures. It's a big herd," Tijo said.

There were deep rumbling sounds now, accompanied by great belches and gusty reports.

"That's their stomachs growling, digesting, and preparing for more food," Tijo explained.

"More food?" Grullo asked eagerly, swinging his head from side to side.

"You think you eat a lot, Grullo." Tijo laughed softly at the big dun-colored stallion. "But one of these bulls eats five times as much as you."

"So you say your people hunt them?" Grullo asked.

"Yes. Their meat is sweeter than most meat and rich. What they don't eat, they cure and eat all through the winter. It fills the belly like no other meat." Tijo paused. "But it takes skill and strong hunters to bring down a single thunder creature. Two brought down are enough to keep a band going through a long winter."

Estrella tossed her head sharply to one side to signal that they would go around the creatures and leave them a wide berth. But she did not hurry. Again, she led them in a soft-hoof walk, something that would not have been possible had they been wearing iron shoes. The herd followed quietly. She blessed the fog that began to roll in again and conceal the first herd's presence. She was grateful that their hooves were naked, that none of them wore shoes. She blessed the nearly invisible moon that hung like a filament of her mane in the sky, and she was thankful that her favorite star had been swallowed by the roiling mist of this darkness. If they could just pass through — unseen, unheard, mute like a ghost herd in the shadows of this night.

Pego was uneasy as he trotted along with the chieftain on his back. They had joined other men of El Miedo's expedition. They were all mounted now. And they were heading toward a vast plain where some of the scouts had seen the tracks of the first herd. He could feel El Miedo's eyes on him the entire time. Pego's mind worked slowly. *He wants me. Will he exact revenge if he captures me?* One thing was certain. He would not be treated like a god, not the way this band of Chitzen treated him. The chieftain had assigned two strong-handed members of the band to massage his muscles every time they returned from a ride. A burr was not allowed to rest for a minute in his mane or tail, as two women meticulously groomed him three times a day with the combs made from bone. Not only that, but the chieftain's mate was ordered to prepare special foods for him. The tastiest was a dish made from the thorny plants. She would strip these plants, then mash the flesh into a creamy pulp. It was a tangy mixture both sweet and sour at the same time, and he was served this dish as if he were a king. The chieftain would spread out a large white blanket. He would sit at one end eating his victuals from a bowl and insisted that a wooden bucket of the mash be set at the other end for Pego. All this would vanish if the chieftain traded him to El Miedo for glass beads and muskets. That could not happen!

But Pego could tell that the chieftain was falling in love with the muskets. When El Miedo had demonstrated how the musket could bring down a deer, the Chitzen had gasped in delight. A shaft of moonlight had fallen on the shiny surface of the musket that was matched only by the gleam in the chieftain's eyes. He wanted that killing stick. And El Miedo, through smiles and gestures of offering, communicated that one would be his if the chieftain would help capture the boy and the first herd. As if magically summoned, a deer had suddenly materialized. El Miedo raised the firing stick, aimed it, and brought down the deer in one shot. Then his men butchered the deer and gave every bit of meat to the Chitzen. From that moment, they were in El Miedo's hands. Pego knew that the musket was the lure. The trap wouldn't take long, for soon the Chitzen would be slaves and the muskets trained on them.

Hours later, Estrella breathed a sigh of relief. She had successfully led her herd around the thunder creatures, and now the horses were taking a well-deserved rest under the shade of a large tree. Within a few minutes, she fell sound asleep, her legs locked in the slumbering posture. Yazz stood next to her surveying the landscape, while the others indulged in their favorite ways to relax. Grullo rolled in the dirt, letting out little snorts as he scratched his back. Angela and Corazón stood head to tail, grooming each other.

Hope watched all this from a thicket of sagebrush. He had followed the horses around the thunder creatures and knew they were weary. If there was ever a time to strike, this was it. Yet he knew now that he could not seek vengeance. His father's soul was lost. There was nothing he could do to save him, and most important, Little Coyote knew that he would never be haunted by him. He was done with hiding, with spying on this herd. Hope was determined to become a part of something, something good. He came out from behind the thicket and took his first step toward that something. Just at that moment, the air split as a loud, sharp crack reverberated across the plains.

"Guns!" roared Arriero, who'd spent enough time in battle to recognize the sound.

Hope froze. The Ibers were far behind them. Or so he had thought. Could they have followed the herd unseen?

"Men and guns!" Bobtail's shrill whinny cut through a thunderous pounding that could never have come from men and horses alone. It was something else . . .

Hold On tossed his head and flared his nostrils to sift through the scents swirling through the charged air. "The Ibers are close. They're hunting the thunder creatures."

Estrella now saw them. Dusty figures in the dawn, hundreds of Ibers were mounted on horses and mules, and Chitzen on foot followed, thinking they were on a grand hunt for enough meat to get them through the winter.

For a moment, Estrella couldn't move. She couldn't speak. Two terrible words echoed through her head: *I've failed*. The *omo* owl had been right. She should have split the herd. And now it was too late.

Then the pounding of the massive creatures became deafening. It was as if the earth were convulsing. The other horses snorted anxiously, their eyes wide with fear and confusion as they looked to Estrella, waiting for her to tell them what to do. But all she could do was stare at the cloud of dust rising up from the horizon.

"Stampede!" Tijo yelled as he leapt onto Estrella's back. But his voice was lost in the concussion of noise as over a thousand thunder creatures raced in panic. Like a turbulent dark river the immense animals streamed across the plains.

Tijo leaned forward and shouted in Estrella's ears, "Stay away from the middle. Get to the edges." They could smell the sweat of the beasts. And cutting through that odor of sweat was the acrid smell of gunpowder.

Guns! Hold On thought. *Guns! I thought we had left those far, far behind.* Hold On ran shoulder to shoulder with Estrella.

"We must split into two groups," Yazz whinnied, before she realized she must save her breath. No one could hear her in the midst of this maelstrom of noise, fear, and guns — for the guns kept firing. She could hardly see, for the thunder creatures had kicked up a blizzard of dust. Even breathing was hard, and with each breath they inhaled more dust than air. She heard a hacking near her. It was Hold On. Poor Hold On, whose lungs had been scraped with smoke in the canyon fire and his eyes singed into darkness. Would he now finally succumb? Yazz heard the grand old stallion stumble. But he was up again, his voice rasping. The thud of his hooves seemed like a drummer's beat in a march and beneath them a refrain: *I shall not yield . . . I shall not yield.*

Estrella heard that beat as well. The beat from the stallion's hooves began to reverberate through the herd. The old horse's astonishing determination despite the clamor seemed to travel through the herd. They would not be captured. They would sooner be blown to bits by musket fire.

Is it possible? Estrella thought. *Are we gaining speed? Will we escape?*

Then there seemed to be a clearing in the dust at the very center of the herd. A whiteness rose that was not dust at all as the pelt of the darkest of the thunder creatures began to fade. At first, it turned pale yellow. But it grew whiter and whiter. Tijo now realized he had felt her presence, Haru's spirit, ever since they had arrived on the plains. The huge white creature turned its enormous head. The eyes on either side fixed him in its gaze. Haru! She had found a new spirit lodge!

Go east,
Go west.
Guns and men
They shall enslave
And this will be your living grave.

But it was too late. Estrella heard two words over the din: "*¡Adelante! ¡Adelante!*" It was the voice of an Iber. Then a peculiar whistling seared the air. Like a snarl of vipers, something writhed above her and Tijo's heads. Then she felt the sting as two lassos fell upon them. There was the sudden burning of the rope on her neck and then the cinching. She twisted violently, crashing to the ground. Tijo felt himself yanked from her back, then reeled in like a fish.

From her spirit lodge, Haru looked on in horror. She knew in that same moment that she had quickly worn out this lodge of the thunder creature. She had tried to reach beyond the shelter of the immense creature. A spirit housed within the body of another animal could only see a story about to happen, tell a story, but had no power to control that story. The spirit in that sense was powerless. She had tried to control the story. She must return to the spirit camps perhaps forever.

PART 2

A New Lodge

CHAPTER 9

Pego Reflects

Estrella fought them all the way back to the Ibers' camp. A chain twitch clamped down painfully across her upper lip and restricted the movements of her whole head. There were now three ropes around her neck, and the Ibers were trying to get close enough to hobble one of her front hooves to her back hoof, but she kept bucking and whinnying. Her eyes rolled into her head. She crashed to the ground, and before she could get up, they had secured the hobbles just above her fetlocks. Then more ropes, until finally eight Ibers were actually dragging her into the stall. The last thing she recalled was the slam of the stall door and the sound of the bolt lock. She lay there in the suffocating, airless darkness for quite a while in a state of shock. The wall seemed to lean in on her. There was no sky, no stars, no moon nor sun. It was like the ship hold she had been foaled in, except there was no dam. No Perlina.

At last when she got up, she found that the hobble on her feet had loosened. There was no longer a twitch, but she had three ropes around her neck looped through iron rings on the stall walls. She began panting again. There was not enough air to breathe, and the darkness closed in around her.

She was dying. And she had only herself to blame. Her impatience had ruled her, owned her, and led her into this disaster. If only she had stopped and listened when the *omo* owl appeared. Then painfully she recalled Bella's words: "Have faith, young'un. We all have faith in you." The very word *faith* had made her flinch. And now she knew she'd been right. She did not deserve anyone's faith.

But what had happened to the herd? She and Tijo were the only ones taken to the camp, which meant the others had probably escaped. But were they together, safe? Or had they scattered during the stampede and were now wandering apart, scared and lost and alone? Her heart ached as she thought about Hold On sniffing the air for signs of his friends.

The walls of the stall pressed tighter. Her heart raced. The panting seized her again. She must concentrate on breathing normally, deep long breaths, not the shallow ones that seemed to scrape at her lungs. She must quell the panic that was threatening to suffocate her.

She stood very quietly for a long while, and eventually

realized that she was not alone. Pego was in the next stall. She recognized his scent. Oddly, she was not angry or fearful. She would not waste fear on him.

But she was fearful for Tijo. Where was he? She couldn't smell him. What would they do to him? Enslave him as they had the Chitzen? They, too, were in fetters. She'd heard their wailing and seen them placed in a pen. El Miedo had taken them as slaves just as the Seeker had done to the Chitzen of the south. How would Tijo fare as a slave among slaves, people who already had hated him? Would their hatred for him deepen now that he was more horse than human?

Estrella heard footsteps approaching. She knew the scent immediately. El Miedo. He smelled of the spirit liquids that she remembered from her time on the ship, the strange drink that made the men behave crazy at times. There was also sweat. Human sweat was different from that of animals with fur. It was stronger, saltier. She had only encountered this man El Miedo two times, once months before at the ravine when they had jumped, and then when she had been roped and dragged into the stall. He had stood by gloating as they had hobbled her hind feet. Although, at first, she didn't recognize his language, he had stood there making strange triumphant hooting sounds as they had finally attached her hobbled feet to a stake. He was taking great pleasure in seeing her vanquished, actually clapping his hands with delight. At one point, he tripped near her hind leg, which she tried to lash out to kick him. But of course she couldn't. He delighted in her failure. Stepping around to her head, he drew his face close to hers. The stench of his breath was awful. His eyes like dark agates bore into her.

His brow knotted as he spoke. His thick mustache twitched as if it had a life of its own. The Iber language, which she'd learned as a tiny foal on the ship, began to come back to her. She knew what he was saying. "I shall break you, and if I don't break you, I shall crush you." She peeled back her lips, and a sound she never knew she could make slithered out — a long, low hiss like that of a snake. He looked startled, then suddenly his fist smashed her muzzle. She saw the blood on his knuckles. Her blood. He turned away, delighted.

The indignation was worse than the pain. She, who was born wild, was now subject to the whims and cruelty of men. She could not bear it. She spun around and kicked the stall in frustration, hoping to feel it shatter under her hooves.

Next to her, El Miedo was addressing Pego. "So, my friend, we meet again, eh? Our last encounter — well, how should I put it? — was a bit rough." There was a long pause. "And now look at you. All four legs hobbled to posts. I doubt you will ever throw me again. Humiliate me in front of my troops again, you cowardly beast!" Estrella heard a thud, the same sound of his fist smashing a horse's face. Pego's. But Pego did not emit a single whinny.

"I called you a mule then, and that is what you are and

shall be from now on. You see, I plan to build a road. A road to El Dorado. There is gold in this country. I can smell it. I shall find the gold and build a road, for there will be cartload after cartload of gold. And you, my friend, shall help me build that road. You shall be yoked and learn to work in the jerkline with the other mules and the humans I've captured. You like that? You . . . you . . . *Pura Raza*." He spat out the two words as he spun on his heel and strode away.

Once El Miedo left, only silence followed. A deep, thick silence that was finally broken by Estrella.

"We are all to be slaves, then," she said.

"He said nothing about you," Pego replied flatly. The pride in his voice had disappeared, and Estrella could sense that something inside him had broken.

"If Tijo is a slave, then I shall be as good as enslaved myself. If he is yoked, I am yoked."

Estrella knew that Pego could not understand that. He could not comprehend that kind of bond between two living things. That souls could be bound to one another in a manner that did not always require chains. She would never be free until Tijo was free. She did not even know where Tijo was being held, but there was one thing she did know — neither she nor Tijo would let El Miedo break them. Somehow, they would escape. She had Tijo to live for, the herd to live for. Pego had nothing.

CHAPTER 10

Torn

They had not split, yet the herd felt as if their heart had been ripped out. The horses were snorting and trembling as they milled about confusedly on the edge of the plains. The thunder creatures had gone, leaving nothing but trampled grass and despair in their wake.

"But are you sure, Hold On?" Angela asked frantically. "Are you really sure that they got Estrella and Tijo? How? How could that have happened?"

"I don't know. I just heard the rope fall on Estrella, then a second later on Tijo, and they were gone. Just gone!"

Grullo broke in with a shaky voice. "I saw Estrella fall to the ground. I saw the rope around her neck and one on Tijo's shoulders. He flew into the air. He could have been trampled — more easily than Estrella."

They all shuddered as the horrible image loomed in their minds.

"They can't be gone," Verdad the colt said, dancing nervously from side to side. "I mean . . . I mean . . ." But his words dwindled off. The three stallions, Grullo, Bobtail, and Arriero, were wheezing and giving fretful whinnies.

Hold On understood their confusion. The idea of Estrella — the freest, wildest horse any of them had ever known — bound in ropes and chains was impossible to imagine, like trying to picture the night sky without stars.

No one spoke for a long time. Hold On stood trembling in the dusky light of a pine forest. Grullo, the steady old stallion, came up and began to run his muzzle across Hold On's withers.

"They are gone, aren't they?" Hold On whispered.

"Yes. They are gone but not forever. They will find their way home."

"Forever for one as old as myself doesn't matter, as my time is short now on this earth. But I don't want to be on this earth without Estrella. I might as well be dead."

"Don't talk this way, Hold On."

"I was running beside them, Grullo. I could not see the lassos fall, but I heard them. I felt them as though they were around my own neck." Hold On gave a shiver. Yes, he could feel the rope. He could hear the shrill scream of his dear Estrella. Tijo's guttural shriek as if his insides were being ripped out. He drooped his head mournfully. Would he never feel the comforting weight of the boy Tijo on his back, or hear the fleet hooves of Estrella next to him? He knew that filly so well. He knew the sound of her heart beating, the rhythm of her swift legs devouring distances.

"We have to go back," Grullo nickered softly. "We must go back and look for them. They might be there still, and hurt, badly hurt."

"Go back," Angela replied. It was not a question but more an exhalation. "Yes, we must."

But none of them moved. Instead, they bunched closer together for comfort.

There was a silence of several seconds. Then Hold On lifted his head and stretched out his neck as if hearing something.

"What's that?" Verdad whinnied, and began to walk toward where he thought Hold On must have heard a sound. A small figure appeared in a thin slant of moonlight.

"It's a coyote," Grullo whispered nervously.

Hope approached the horses quietly, regarding them with wonder and envy. He could tell they were anxious, but there was still something so beautiful about the way they were trying to calm one another.

The horses froze and stiffened when they caught Hope's scent. Yazz, who had been grooming Corazón, felt the old mare go rigid. They were about to flee. Fight or flight. But it could be neither.

"Please don't go," Hope said plaintively. "I wish you no harm. I am not like my father."

Although Hold On could hardly see the small figure quivering before them, he could sense its anguish. Hold On could hear the beat of the small creature's racing heart. His bones almost seemed to rattle. But not only that, the little fellow radiated an overwhelming loneliness of spirit. It was as if he were the most forsaken creature on earth.

A few of the horses tossed their heads nervously and prepared to gallop away from the little coyote, for he brought to them terrible memories.

"Don't leave," Hold On cautioned them in a fierce voice.

Hold On stepped forward and dropped his head, flaring his nostrils. He was experiencing a very peculiar sensation. "I smell your grief."

He lowered his head and touched his muzzle to Hope's head. This touch was so strange, Hope almost leapt to the side in surprise, but then a feeling of calm stole over him. *I am being groomed*, Hope thought. He had never been touched so in his life.

"I am Hope." He looked up into Hold On's sightless eyes. For some reason, when Hope looked up, he felt that the old gray stallion could see right through him and believed what he had said that Hope was not like his father.

"*Es un milagro*," Corazón whispered.

The very word *milagro*, miracle, had an almost mystical effect on the horses. There was complete stillness. Even the crickets of this summer night ceased beating their wings. Each member of the first herd had one thought. *There is still time for miracles.* And they all gathered closer to the coyote called Hope.

"You . . . you are nothing like your father. We thought all coyotes were alike," Grullo said.

"Can we help you?" Angela said, lowering her head for a closer look at the strange creature.

"I think I'm supposed to help you, but I'm not sure how. The owl told me I had a task to perform." The horses exchanged surprised looks. They knew the owl had to be Haru.

"What do you know about the men who took our friends?" Angela asked. "Can you help us find them?"

"I'm not sure," Hope said, looking from Angela to the rest of the herd. "I want to, but I don't know how."

"We should all rest," Hold On said wearily. "Hope, you may stay with us, if you'd like."

Hope blinked in disbelief. Was he really asking him to stay? To be part of something? He was torn. How he would love to join their sleeping circle! But he knew the time wasn't right. Something was drawing him to return to that terrible field, the scene of the stampede. He turned his head and looked at them. "I wish I could stay, but there is something first I must do. I promise I'll come back, and I hope I can help you."

Hold On nodded. "Off you go, then. You are welcome to return whenever you'd like. If the owl chose you to help us, you must truly have a special destiny. Haru hasn't been wrong yet." He let out a sigh, thinking of the warning they had chosen not to heed.

As Hope proceeded, he could hardly see beyond his muzzle through the thickness of the fog. He knew that he was not being simply drawn but called. The words of the owl came back to him: "It means you might be called." He was not sure what he must do to help the horses to bring back their leader, Estrella, and Tijo. But he was sure that his mission would be revealed on that plain. Something awaited him, something that would prepare him for his task. *My task,* he thought. *My mission. My calling.*

The world had become deeply mysterious to the coyote, spilling with perplexing secrets and unexplainable riddles. Hope was not sure how he was finding his way. But his feet seemed to take him forward as the mist swirled around him. He began to experience a strange lightness, as if he might be floating, caught on the current of a swiftly moving river with a secret destination. Ahead, he spotted a small glow of radiance. It grew larger, and then suddenly he knew that he had arrived.

"Here! I am here."

"Yes," a familiar voice replied.

"Grace?"

"Indeed."

"Grace, I can smell flowers." The coyote inhaled deeply.

"I told you I would see you again when the *Gilia sinuata* blooms." At just that moment, Hope heard a shuddering hoot of an owl overhead. Then came a thumping like a huge beast.

"Don't be afraid," Grace said, and landed on Hope's shoulder. A great white mass of a thunder creature was making its way slowly toward Hope, limping or was it staggering, its burden too heavy? What could be too heavy for such an enormous beast?

"What is happening?" Hope asked. Hope suddenly felt very strange. It was as if the edges of his being, the borders between his body and the rest of the world, were dissolving. Then the *omo* owl melted out of the mists. Two white creatures and one like a tiny rainbow faced Hope.

"Hope," the *omo* owl began to speak. "We have all been called. We have all served."

"You are next," the thunder creature said softly.

"Next? Next to die?"

"No, not at all. You are my next spirit lodge." It was the same voice that had flowed from the *omo* owl. "Haru cannot use me anymore. My lodge is too weary. To shift from such a small lodge to a very large one sometimes makes that new lodge wear thin faster. I stumbled, and alas Tijo and Estrella were caught. No, you must try as a spirit lodge for me. Together we can try."

"Try what?"

"To rescue Tijo and Estrella."

The mists had started to clear, and Hope felt the press of moonlight against his face. He began to have the sensation of becoming lighter and lighter. It seemed as if his body were evaporating, and yet he had never felt more alive.

"What is happening to me?"

"You are growing. My spirit, the spirit of Haru, auntie-mother of Tijo, is filling you. I was allowed to return from the spirit camps even though I have worn out so many lodges, the lodge of *omo* owl, the lodge of a thunder creature. You will house me now. You are my lodge."

The *omo* owl and the white thunder creature were now like wisps of vanishing fog. "You are the long spirits. You and Estrella and Tijo — long spirits stretching back in time to the very beginnings — the time before time. Go now. You have work to do."

And then they were gone.

"Grace? Grace? Are you still here?"

There was a flickering of color.

"Yes, dear, but I must be off. I'll see you when the *Aurora salix* blooms."

"*Aurora salix?*"

"The dawn willow."

For a moment, the world seemed to hold its breath. The

wind grew still and the stars grew brighter. Something rare, something vast and hugely complicated seemed to be happening within him. Hope whispered into the night, "I have a friend . . . I have a spirit . . . Life has become more than I ever thought. Life is miraculous!"

CHAPTER 11

To Deceive a Deceiver

It had been only a short time since Hope had gone through the odd transformation of becoming a spirit lodge. He did not feel all that different although he knew he was larger and his yellowish pelt had turned a silvery shade of gray. When he returned to the first herd as the sun was rising, they did not shy away as he had expected them to. The horses could tell that he was still Hope, just somehow slightly altered. Hold On's nostrils flared, and he inhaled deeply. Then he cocked his head from side to side as if searching for that old familiar scent.

"I know it's you," Hold On said.

"Yes, just a little different."

The spirit of Haru was an amicable presence within him.

Although he was sheltering her spirit, Hope felt sheltered himself. Perhaps it was because Haru had been a mother. He had never really known what a mother was like. But now he felt the warmth, the nurturing warmth of a female flowing through him. He was aware of an extraordinary tenderness combined with a fierceness that was strange and compelling. It was as if he had become a container of all things, a world for all things. *I am truly a spirit lodge!*

Hold On walked up very close to him and lowered his head so his muzzle was nearly touching Hope's. With his clouded eyes, he peered deeply into Hope's clear green eyes. *The blind one sees all*, Hope thought.

Now finally the words came to Hope. "I am going to help Estrella and Tijo."

"But, dear," Angela said softly. "How can you help? You are small and young. These Ibers are vicious."

Without taking his eyes from Hope, the old stallion began to speak. "Hope is right. He has one skill that his father had. You see, Hope, the time has come for you to slip into other creatures' minds."

Hope was aghast. "Time for me to become the dream stealer? The fantastic concealer? Never!"

"*¡Calma, calma!*" Hold On soothed him in the language of the Ibers. "You are not becoming this. It is a pretense. To conceal, to be deceitful is not your true nature. It will never be."

"But . . ."

"You can do this, Hope. To rescue Estrella and Tijo, you can do this. Did your father ever do anything with good intentions?" Hope shook his head. "I am not asking that you trick Estrella or Tijo, but El Miedo, who is as terrible an Iber as ever crossed the ocean from the Old Land to this New Land. And although your father used this skill in malice, you shall use it in love and redeem the evils of your father, make right all that was wrong, make goodness out of depravity. For you are a long spirit. I feel that spirit within you."

Hold On paused and emitted a deep sigh, a weary sigh. "To deceive a deceiver — is that so bad?"

"No. Not at all," Hope replied. His voice was strong and resolute. *This*, he thought, *is Haru speaking.* And in truth, it did infuse him with a kind of courage he never suspected he possessed.

I can slip into others' minds. How strange, Hope thought. *What will it feel like? How will I know what to do?* But then he realized that it would not be just him who would slip into their minds but Haru as well. And this gave him great comfort. *She is with me,* he thought.

Of course I am, a voice seemed to resonate in his head. *I believe as Hold On said that you are a long spirit like Estrella, like Tijo.*

He thought about all of this as he made his way toward the growing encampment of El Miedo.

Now as the coyote drew closer, he sensed precisely where Estrella and Tijo were. Estrella was certainly not kept in the corral that had been erected, nor was Pego. They had been put in a newly built stable with only two stalls. Tijo was jailed in a separate smaller enclosure a good distance from the stable.

A guard with a musket was posted on each side of the large corral. *They are guarding against wolves*, thought Hope. Soft cluckings came from a low roofed structure. The chicken house. How his father had loved raiding the chicken houses of the Ibers. Across from the corral, he heard the clink of metal. He soon realized the sound came from chains. In the dusky light, he saw Chitzen moving about slowly inside another enclosure. There were the cries of children and the low mumble of several adults. They were all tethered in one way or another to posts. The tethers were long but not long enough. They could only walk a short distance from a scattering of tents and a brush arbor that had been hastily built to protect them from the sun during the day or the rare rain at this time of year.

There was another small unfinished building that housed neither animals nor people. It, too, had a brush roof supported by four poles but no walls. Beneath it was a raised platform with a statue of a pretty lady. A man knelt in front of her, murmuring words. Hope slinked through the gathering shadows of the night. He knew that he had lost his scent entirely. Moving undetected was easy. Even his paws did not seem to leave a track. Perhaps this was all part of serving a spirit — becoming a lodge for another soul. No one noticed him: not the Chitzen, not the musket-bearing guards, not the padre who knelt mumbling in front of the pretty wooden lady.

He had not gone far, his silvery pelt blending in perfectly with the night. Then he heard the snores from what was obviously El Miedo's tent, for it flew the red flag with the crown of the Iber monarchy. Hope crept past the guard, who was luckily sleeping, to a back corner of the tent and slipped under the canvas. The canvas smelled of salt, and although Hope had never seen the ocean, he seemed instinctively to know that the canvas had been made from the sails that had brought these strange humans to the New Land. He settled himself beneath the cot of El Miedo and felt a dark shadow flow from him. It looked so much like his own father, yet he was not afraid.

The shadow settled just above El Miedo's head, and the man stirred in his sleep. He turned over onto his back. His mouth gaped. He began to mumble some sort of incantation or prayer. The Ibers did a lot of praying, but El Miedo seemed to be swallowing the shadow. Then he murmured, "*Gracias, viejo amigo. ¡Volviste!*" Thank you, old friend. You have come back! *He feels*, Hope realized, *that my father has come back to help him*. But this time the dream that swirled in El Miedo's mind was slightly different. Before, he had dreamed of power and the magnificent dark horse of destiny. He now dreamed of a shining nugget of gold. Pure gold. And Big Coyote would help him find it.

Tijo sat with his knees pulled to his chest in the small shelter. There was a stake in the ground with a chain, and that chain was attached to a metal cuff on Tijo's ankle. In the three days he had been a prisoner of El Miedo, he had examined every link of that chain, trying to figure out how to escape. There was one opening in the shed but it, too, had metal on it. Metal bars. A prison guard came in now and drove the stake farther into the ground and checked the lock. Tijo observed him carefully. The man's sly eyes crawled over him.

"You think you can get loose, boy? Well, you can't . . . Oooh, and I have a nice little surprise for you." Tijo did not understand a word he said. He saw the man go over to the door and pick up a yoke. "Now try this on for size." He placed it over Tijo's head so it set on his shoulders. "Perfect fit!" He brought his face close to Tijo's. "You're going to work the jerkline. You're no more Horse Boy. You're a mule boy!"

When the guard left, Tijo dropped his head to his knees. The rough wood of the yoke scraped his shoulders, and he let out a low cry. Until now, his capture had seemed like a nightmare from which he'd surely awake, but now there was no denying the terrible truth. He'd lost the herd, the only home he'd ever known. But although he knew only pain and despair awaited him, he worried more for Estrella than for himself. He knew what it was like to be alone. After Haru died, there'd been no one in the world who cared what happened to him. But Estrella had never been parted from her herd, never been subjected to the cruelty of humans.

He was trying to adjust the yoke when he spied the skulking shadow of a coyote outside. A silvery gray shadow nimbly slipped through the bars. Tijo's despair melted away. He did not even feel the weight of the yoke. Joy flooded through him. He knew that Haru was with him.

"You have found a new spirit lodge," he said with a smile.

"Yes, the coyote Hope. And he is your Hope in more than name." Her voice blew through like a soft breeze. The coyote crept close to him, and Tijo felt a radiance issuing from her. It was love. Her eyes blinked and shimmered with tears as the coyote nuzzled his cheek, just as Haru used to do.

"Now listen and obey." There was a quaver in her voice that he had never heard before. The coyote raised his paw. It was almost exactly like the times Haru raised her finger to scold him when he was naughty as a child. "Remember you are Horse Boy. You, like Estrella, are a long spirit." And in that moment, Tijo saw the sparkly little horse hovering just above the coyote's ears. The prison suddenly seemed crowded with good spirits.

"Tomorrow, the padre will come to you, to show you the ways of his god and to bless you. Go . . . go willingly. Make yourself smile as if you understand every word." Tijo nodded vigorously, as he felt a tide of hope rising within him. He wasn't alone. He had Haru, and she would help him and Estrella return to their herd. "Now listen carefully." Tijo nodded again eagerly. "When the moment comes, you and Estrella will be able to escape."

Hope left as quietly as he had entered and then slipped into the stable, where Estrella had finally managed to fall asleep. The lacerations on her neck and shoulders were raw from the lasso that had snagged her. She stood lightly, favoring one leg, but they were all hobbled. It had only been three days, but she seemed to have shrunk and grown thinner. Her hip bones stuck out at sharp angles. Even though she appeared to be sleeping, her mouth hung open as if she were gasping for breath.

Hope did not wake her but glided into her dreams — dreams of utter despair. He caught fragments of them. There was the roll of a sea, then a sudden flash of white and the sea turned red with blood. Turbulent dreams of pain and loss and chaos and fire. But suddenly, as Hope wandered this dreamscape, the filly stirred and a sense of calm enveloped everything.

When Estrella would awake the next morning, she would

know for certain that Haru had found a new spirit lodge in the coyote called Hope. She would know exactly where Tijo was imprisoned. The filly sensed that their long spirits, hers and Tijo's, were entangled once again. It was as Haru had once said — long spirits were in essence time weavers. They wove between the oceans of time like the shuttle of her loom. Hope was now the shuttle.

CHAPTER 12

Gods and Gold

Unlike Estrella, El Miedo awoke depleted and distraught from his dreams. It felt as if his mind had been licked by flames of despair, yet right at the very heart of those flames, a golden nugget had shimmered. This had to be a sign that his premonition of gold was real. But what was God demanding of him? He would have to call the padre. Before he could collect the gift God wanted to bestow upon him, he needed to make himself worthy.

And so the padre was summoned.

"Father Alonso," he said as the plump padre came into his tent. "I fear that I have been negligent in our divine offices." The padre's eyes opened wide with a mixture of surprise and delight. "I feel . . ." El Miedo searched for the right words. "I feel that we are on the brink of a marvelous gift from the Holy Mother." He nodded at the statue of the Virgin that was perched on a trunk. A trunk he hoped to fill with gold. "I think that although the building of our chapel is far from finished, we need to consecrate the spot where it shall be on the plaza."

The padre clapped his hands together and tipped his face toward heaven. "Oh, praise God! Don Cristobal, I am thrilled with your decision."

"But not only that. I think we need to begin with the conversion of the Chitzen and a blessing for the animals. For they are all our flock."

"Yes, Don Cristobal. Yes. You shall be blessed for your thoughts. You are not only our fearless leader but a gentle shepherd of this flock."

"Excellent. Then I think we should begin immediately."

An hour later, Tijo was forcing himself to smile broadly up at the padre on the newly constructed plaza. His metal cuff had been removed, as had the yoke he had worn through the night. He glanced over to the horses that were being brought forward two by two, led by bridles and ropes. Tijo gasped when he saw Estrella, with her head imprisoned in that contraption of leather straps. No one led Estrella. She was the leader. Their leader. She was the very core, the heart of the first herd. But she did not seem to be fighting the bridle or the bit. In fact, she seemed almost calm. She, too, must have been visited by the spirit lodger.

Estrella spotted the statue of the Virgin ahead. It brought back memories — memories of the crossing to this new land, for there had been a carved statue similar to this one in the hold of the ship. Just before they were thrown overboard, another padre, Padre Luis, had come to bless the horses. Now they were going to be blessed along with the Chitzen. Did the Iber feel that every evil deed could be erased by a prayer? Estrella looked over at Tijo, who was directly across from her in the line of Chitzen. She could tell they were both thinking the same thing. *There will be a moment. We must be patient, but it will come and then we must break away.* Tijo was not that far from her. One quick leap, and he could make it onto her back. A current of energy ran through her muscles as she imagined how it would feel to gallop again.

The padre was mumbling a prayer. Estrella turned to the mare next to her. "You know the tongue of the Ibers. What is the padre saying?"

"*Libre*, free."

"They are freeing us?" Estrella could see that Tijo was listening. He could understand the mare, too. They both exchanged a glance. Tijo moved himself into a slightly better position. No one seemed to notice. He moved again. He was now right beside the mare that Estella was conversing with. The mare moved just a bit and made room for Tijo to slip between her and Estrella as she continued talking.

"I don't know. I don't really know what the word *free* means anymore." The mare sighed. "But the padre says that we must take our steps to the altar freely, of our own free will if we are to receive the blessings of the Virgin and the Holy Father above."

"So can you tell me," Estrella asked, "what this padre will do so we can receive the blessing?"

"Oh, it's just the blessing of the animals. You see they are even bringing the chickens up as well as the dogs. When the padre calls us, we'll one by one walk forward. Then he will sprinkle holy water on our heads."

"But someone will be holding our reins!"

"No. They drop the reins. That's what I think freely means — without rein."

"And what about the Chitzen?"

"I think it should be the same. Of course, they have the guards with the killing sticks. They can always kill if a creature tries to run."

Estrella looked up. She saw the guards perched on tall ladders with their killing sticks pointed down at them. "They bless and they kill?"

The mare nodded. "Yes, that is the way it is with the Ibers."

Tijo and Estrella exchange a glance. They were in agreement. Neither of them planned to be blessed *or* killed.

It seemed almost miraculous, but the mare had been right. The horses and the Chitzen both advanced to the altar at the same time side by side. As each horse approached, the tethers were dropped.

Closer and closer Estrella and Tijo came. They could smell the desert flowers that festooned the altar. They could see clearly the pretty face of the Virgin even though the blue paint for her eyes was chipped, making her appear half-blind. Estrella was trembling in anticipation. Tijo was a scant distance from her, and she knew that within a few seconds, she would feel the weight of him leaping onto her back. They would be gone!

The rope dropped. The padre began his prayer.

"Benedictus es, Domine Deus, conditor omnium animalium. Vos autem sicut pisces maris et volatilibus caeli et bestiis terrae." Blessed art Thou, O Lord God, the Creator of all living things . . . the fishes of the sea and the fowl of the air and the beasts of the earth you rule.

There was a slight commotion, a mule brayed, and a skittish mare shied. Then Tijo seemed to soar through the air, landing as lightly as a fly on Estrella's back. Estrella reared and, wheeling around, charged from the throng to be blessed. The padre fell over. The Chitzen froze in stunned disbelief.

Estrella, with Tijo on her back, leapt over the altar, knocking off the statue of the pretty lady. The crack of gunfire fractured the air. Straight ahead, five Ibers ran out waving their arms, trying to block Estrella and Tijo's escape. She leapt over them, clearing the tallest with ease. There was one building ahead but no men with firearms. *We'll make it. We'll make it.* Then, again, there was the familiar terrifying hiss. A black scrawl in the clear blue sky. The fierce burn as the rope rasped against flesh, slicing right through her pelt. She crumpled to the ground. Tijo was beside her.

It's over, she thought.

The coyote called Hope staggered as he watched unnoticed at the far edge of the encampment. *It didn't work. We tried so hard.*

It is not the end, the voice of Haru resonated within him *Sometimes, we must fail before we can succeed. Do not abandon hope.*

But looking at the frantic horse flailing on the ground, all he felt was despair.

It was with a heavy heart that Hope made his way back to the first herd. As soon as they glimpsed him returning, a dreadful foreboding stirred among them. Hope stood quietly in front of Hold On as the others crowded around. "It didn't work," he said dejectedly.

"You mean Estrella is still . . . still, and Tijo?" Hold On's withers flinched, and his voice cracked as he spoke.

"Yes," Hope said in a small voice.

Yazz stepped forward. "You tried." They were by a swale of bunch grass. Tiny desert finches flitted in and out, catching insects that normally would have distracted the horses, but a mournful silence had descended on the herd. A few of the finches would land momentarily on the horses' backs or hindquarters, but they did not even swish their tails to clear them away.

"Oh, I did try," Hope said bitterly. "I am not much of a dream stealer or a fantastic concealer. Though I did steal into El Miedo's sleep."

"And what did he dream of, Hope?" Hold On asked in a flat voice.

"Glory and failure and . . . and gold."

"Gold!" Hold On replied as he shoved his ears forward, suddenly alert. "There's your answer, Hope."

"What do you mean?"

"We must tempt him with gold." His filmy eyes almost sparkled.

"Gold? I think that is why he wanted to bless the animals. He thought it would earn him favor with his gods, and the gods would somehow lead him to gold."

"The Iber gods can't show him. But you can."

"But I have no notion of where gold can be found." Hope felt something shift within him. Then a soft jolt deep inside. The spirit had stirred in its lodge. It was as if a hidden eye had opened inside Hope. He was seeing what the spirit of Haru had seen in her previous lodge, that of the *omo* owl. A bright gold nugget lay beneath the ice of a frozen creek. *But how could there still be ice?* Hope wondered. It was late summer now. *It was winter then,* a voice in his head said. *Go find it!*

But how? How can I find it? The omo *owl is not here. The owl is no longer your lodge.*

The old lodge wore thin. The knowledge does not. I am with you still. What I spied high above in flight might be there.

What did you spy — gold?

Fool's gold. And Hope felt the spirit laugh inside him.

Hold On could feel a change in Hope. "You see the gold, don't you?"

"I think so. Or rather it is the spirit that sees."

"Good!" Hold On replied. "Now listen to me — all of you! I have a plan. Even if Hope finds the nugget, the gold alone will not be enough. There must be another lure, as irresistible as gold."

"Like what?" Corazón asked.

"Us." Arriero the dark bay stallion stepped forward.

"Us?" several of the horses repeated, exchanging worried glances.

"No. Not all of us," Yazz said. "But some of us. Arriero especially." The mule looked at the stallion. "Should I tell them or you, Arriero?"

"I will," Arriero said, a distant look in his eyes. "On First Island, there was an auction. Back then, El Miedo did not have the money for the very best horses. He had not found his patron yet. But he wanted me. He was actually the one to name me Arriero the muleteer. The name stuck. He didn't care that I was not a *Pura Raza* like Pego or Centello. What he liked was that I was big. Big with a short back — good for work, but fast as well." Arriero paused. "Eventually, El Miedo found a patron, and being so vain himself, he felt he needed a horse to match the pedigree of his patron Don Esteban, the Duke of Aragon. By then he had enough money to buy all the horses he wanted. He went back to the Seeker, but the Seeker had already won me in the auction, fair and square, and would not sell me." He shook his head. "He was certainly angry then, but in all honesty, I'm sure he hasn't thought of me since."

"You are being too modest, Arriero," Yazz said. "No one could forget you."

"And we can awaken those dreams," Hope said softly. "We can make him remember."

Yazz turned to Hope and fixed him with her large brown eyes. "I think you have perhaps already wakened many dreams where you might not suspect."

"Really?"

"Truly. Didn't the other horses see Estrella and Tijo try to escape?"

"Yes, but how does that help?"

"Though you think your mission failed, Hope, it didn't. You have planted the seeds of freedom in their minds. They will sprout soon."

CHAPTER 13

Awakened Dreams

The mare Abelinda stood off from the other horses in the corral. She was looking at the little mule Mikki, whose back was raw with oozing bloody stripes. *The Ibers would kill that mule before they ever got her in the yoke*, Abelinda thought. Mikki endured their abuse with a calm stubbornness that Abelinda had never seen. It was the mule's very placidity that seemed to anger the men most. It was as if Mikki knew there was something better in this world, but it was not death. How could she believe this? Abelinda wondered. What did she believe?

She kept recalling her strange conversation with the filly Estrella. She'd asked Abelinda what the padre was saying because she did not fully understand the language of the Ibers.

"The padre says that we must take our steps to the altar freely or of our own free will if we are to receive the blessings of the Virgin and the Holy Father above," Abelinda had explained, but she herself had to confess that she did not quite understand the meaning of the word *free*. She felt that she might have once long ago. But she had been bought and sold so many times it was hard to recall what she might have known or learned. Both her mind and her body were owned by the Ibers. It seemed as if it always had and always would be that way. But as Estrella had approached the altar to be blessed, the filly had bolted with the young Chitzen on her back.

Abelinda had been stunned at the time and then rather relieved when they had been caught and brought back. What they had done seemed freakish and dangerous. Now, however, there was this whispering at the back of her mind, this niggling, insistent thought like a flea on her hindquarters that her tail could not swish away. The thought was that something was very wrong, and she should not have felt relief when they brought back the filly and the boy. These feelings all had to do with the strange word *free*.

Abelinda had thought she was too old to carry a foal, but if indeed she did carry one, would they sell it as they had the others she had borne? When Estrella had broken loose, Abelinda had seen a sparkle in the filly's eyes, a sparkle that she had never before seen in any horse's eyes for as long as she could remember. Was there something she should know about, must know about, if she was indeed to foal again?

Abelinda shook the thought away as she watched an Iber lieutenant walking toward the little mule. Like a black snake, a whip hung from the crook of his elbow. Another Iber officer followed with a yoke. Seconds later, she heard the crack of that whip landing on Mikki's back, the mule refusing the yoke. *The yoke . . . the yoke . . . Why would they put a yoke on one that young?*

It was odd, but pieces of these elusive thoughts and this word *free* started to come together. Like a blossom opening in sunlight, meaning slipped into Abelinda's mind — what was unconscious became conscious. The little mule no more than six months old should be free . . . *I should be free . . .* She looked across at the mule, her back slippery with blood. *This is so wrong!* The flower had turned into a flame, and it was burning inside of her.

Jacinto stood a short distance away. He brayed softly toward the mare. He saw something in her eyes like the lick of a small flame growing — a new sense, a revelation. *Freedom!* he thought. It was time to ignite that fire. "How long can this go on?" Jacinto asked.

Abelinda lifted her head and shook it. She saw Jacinto's shoulders tense, his ears lay back. He sprang forward and charged. The Iber lieutenant fell to the ground. Jacinto then wheeled about and bucked. His hoof struck the Iber holding the yoke. Blood spurted. The yoke dropped to the ground. The little mule ran off. A silence fell on the corral, and Abelinda bolted toward the yoke and began stomping on it. The crack of the wood rang in all the animals' ears as loudly as that of the whip. Jacinto and Abelinda looked at each other. They both had the same thought. *The yoke has been broken, and that is the first step.*

The tumult caused by the mules reduced El Miedo's camp to chaos as men were dispatched to fix the fence and retrieve the missing animals. *Perfect!* Hope thought as he slinked into the encampment and settled into a corner of the small cell in which Tijo was curled up, his back to him. *I am watching him through the eyes and the heart of the spirit inside me.* Hope felt the boy's despair, the loss of everything he had come to love and value. Tijo sensed Hope's presence and rolled over, regarding the coyote with the saddest eyes the creature had ever seen. Tijo was looking at him, then through him, trying to find the spirit the coyote harbored. Hope rounded his back and began coughing dryly, just the way the dogs did when coughing up a hair ball. However, it was not a hair ball that came out but instead a bright gold nugget.

"What is this?" Tijo asked wearily.

"It is what all these Ibers lust for — gold."

"But what am I to do with it?"

"Just wait. Trust me."

A few minutes later, Hope slipped into Estrella's stall and coughed up an identical nugget. Then he left, uttering the same words to the same question. "Just wait. Trust me."

Now Hope made his way into the tent of El Miedo. The landscape of this man's dreams was so easy to navigate and to manipulate, "to steal" as Hope's father would say. But the coyote knew it was not his father doing the manipulation now; Haru the spirit was sheltered within him.

Two nuggets you shall behold
That gleam like the brightest gold.
A fool's gold shall lure you forth
And another stallion to the north,
A stallion bold
As good as gold,
A stallion oh so strong,
For whom you have forever longed,
And then there are the rest.
So indeed you shall be thrice blessed!

"It must have been a wolf pack that scared all the mules," one lieutenant said to another.

"Yes, the wolves," the blacksmith said.

In the confusion that had broken out with horses rearing and mules bucking and Ibers flooding into the corral to control the horses, Hope had accomplished what he had set out to do. Plant the seed of lust for gold in El Miedo's mind — all while the animals in the corral were sowing the seeds of freedom.

"¡Todo es calma!" another lieutenant proclaimed when the padre had finished saying a blessing over a dead Iber. And then men had come to remove his body. Somehow, Mikki, who had been the cause of the tumult, had been forgotten entirely. She stood now beside Jacinto, who muttered, "Everything is far from calm, little one."

"But what about Abelinda?" Mikki said. She watched as the mare walked toward a small gathering of horses near the main water trough.

"The time is coming," Jacinto said to Mikki.

And his words were echoed by Abelinda to the horses at the trough. "The time is coming. The time is coming."

"Time for what?" a colt asked.

"You remember the filly Estrella and the boy? You remember what happened in the plaza at the blessing?"

"They tried to run. They were whipped," the colt said.

"They wanted to be . . . free," Abelinda whispered.

"But the Ibers won't give us our freedom," the younger mare replied.

"Of course not! Freedom is not to be given. It is to be taken!" Jacinto snorted forcefully.

The word passed through the corrals. Something was going to happen. They should all be ready. They felt something none of them had ever felt before — a wildness rising in their blood.

Abelinda walked over to the little mule. "Mikki?"

"Yes?"

"Mikki, you stay close to me and be ready."

"Be ready for what?"

"To rid yourself of your yoke forever."

"No yoke!" she replied with delight shining in her eyes. She understood completely, faster than any of the grown-up horses or mules.

El Miedo awoke, and though he could not really remember his dream, he felt an urgency to see the Chitzen boy. As the guard unlocked the door, a thrill coursed through him. The light in the small cell was dim. The boy sat very still in the corner, but both the guard and El Miedo gasped when they saw the gleam of the gold nugget.

"Where? Where did this come from?" he asked, pointing at the gold. But of course the boy did not understand the Iber tongue. So El Miedo began gesticulating madly, pointing at the gold, then sweeping his hands in all directions and repeating the words *"¿Dónde? . . . ¿De dónde proviene este oro?"*

At that moment, another guard broke in, *"¡Capitán! ¡Capitán! Venga, venga."* Come! Come! And then he stopped abruptly as his eyes locked on the gold nugget in Tijo's hand. *"¡Es la misma!"*

"What is the same?"

"La misma pepita de oro." The same gold nugget.

"Where?"

"In the stall of the horse — the filly."

El Miedo suddenly felt dizzy. He looked at the boy, the boy he had beaten and called mule boy. Was this what stood between him and gold?

Then the song from his dream came back to him, threading through his mind.

Two nuggets you shall behold
That gleam like the brightest gold.
A fool's gold shall lure you forth
And another stallion to the north,
A stallion bold
As good as gold,
A stallion oh so strong,
For whom you have forever longed,
And then there are the rest.
So indeed you shall be thrice blessed!

His mouth dropped open in wonder. His old friend Coyote had come back to him. Coyote had come back! He could hardly believe it. He knew he had sensed gold nearby. He knew it had to be very close. And the stallion, the one he had named but could not buy, Arriero was near as well. And the first herd! Such blessings so close.

He raced to Estrella's stall, and there it lay on a pile of straw, burning bright, beckoning him. He looked up into Estrella's eyes. The gold was reflected like a small flame in each of her dark eyes.

"¿Usted y el muchacho me llevarán allí?" You and the boy will take me there, truly?

Estrella, who was starting to remember the Iber tongue, understood what he had said. This would be their chance, and yet it would be even riskier than their first attempt to escape. They would be under heavy guard. Her feet might not be hobbled, but there would be the painful twitch on her nose and she could not imagine what restraints they would put on Tijo. She kept her gaze focused on the gold nugget. A few little sparks seemed to fly from the center. She blinked. The sparks were fusing into one bright form. A small horse was prancing above the gold nugget. Am I the only one who can see this? Estrella wondered. For all the radiance of the gold was dwindling, and yet with each second, the tiny horse grew brighter. But did El Miedo or the guard notice this? Their eyes were fastened on the nugget that had lost its shimmer and become dull and lumpen as a clot of dirt. However, neither one of the men seemed to notice this. Then the sudden fragrance of the sweet grass swept through the close air of the stall. Something was happening, or was about to happen.

"¡Es un milagro!" El Miedo said, bending down to pick up the lump that now looked as dark as coal. Estrella nodded her head gently as if in agreement. And it *was* a miracle of sorts. How could the Ibers be so blind? But she kept her eyes on the tiny horse, which now turned its head and seemed to say, *Fear not, fear not.* Estrella thought of her dam, Perlina. She thought of the star that never moves. Her guide stars were back.

CHAPTER 14

Breaking the *Falange*

They were all there behind a bluff, except Arriero, who was continuing to climb to the crest. The sun gleamed down on his muscular back.

"What do you see?" Hold On nickered.

"They are bringing a lot of horses and mules with carts."

"Carts for the rock veined with gold," Yazz said, blowing gusts of wind through her nostrils in contempt. "I've been on a gold jerkline before. It's pure misery. They need to haul so much rock to find the tiniest bit of gold. It's the hardest labor there is for a mule, pulling those carts of rock. Many die in the harness after short lives."

"And the Chitzen," Arriero added. "I can see from here that they are in chains."

"El Miedo needs slaves to dig for the gold and then later to smash the rocks," Yazz said.

"What about Estrella and Tijo?" Hold On asked. The stallion tossed his head impatiently, as if he himself were trying to cast off an invisible bit and harness.

"I can't spot them yet. But, Yazz, can you come up here? I am not sure what I am seeing. It looks like . . . like . . . a *falange caballo*."

"What?" Sky asked.

"A *falange*," Hold On's voice echoed ominously.

"A *falange*?" Verdad said. "I don't know this word."

"If you've been in battle, you know it," Grullo said. "It means a formation like a locked box."

"Estrella and Tijo must be at the center of the *falange*. Surrounded by the other horses so they cannot escape," Bobtail said.

"And the other horses have riders?" Verdad asked.

"Yes, with pikes and the muskets," Arriero said. Then the stallion tossed his head and whinnied shrilly. "I see Pego!" The other horses spun around, but none could see as far as Arriero, who described what he saw. "I can't tell who's riding him, but it's not El Miedo. Oh! I can see Estrella and Tijo in the very center of the *falange*."

Hold On sighed. "Truly a locked box!"

"We'll see," Arriero said, and began to move so he would be in full view. "We'll see."

Verdad and Sky, the two young colts, exchanged nervous glances. The stallion seemed very calm.

"He's the lure," Sky said as he watched Arriero climb the slope. "He and the gold are the lure. But the gold is nowhere. And now he is standing right there on the crest. They can see him plainly. How can he be so calm?"

"War," whispered Hold On. "He's been in war. War hardens."

Arriero open his mouth and whinnied. The cry unfurled on the breeze.

"There he is!" El Miedo whispered, his voice quivering with anticipation as he caught sight of the magnificent stallion. "Fall in and lock!"

Pego, who was being ridden by a lowly sergeant, looked at Jacinto. "That's a battle command. Who's the enemy here?" Pego asked, confused.

"The enemy is within," Jacinto replied, glancing at Estrella. As soon as the command was given to fall in and lock, the mule felt the press of the horses surrounding him.

"What?" Pego asked. "Are we heading for battle?"

"No, not a battle. Not yet. El Miedo is protecting the center of the *falange*. He doesn't want the filly or the boy to escape," Jacinto said. El Miedo sensed that the filly and the boy held a precious secret, a secret about gold. Estrella and the boy were both his enemy and his salvation.

A current of tension ran through the *falange*. Jacinto gave a sharp glance to Abelinda, warning her to say nothing. The horses, the mules were ready. And who knew if Pego, too, might be ready, yet Jacinto would never trust him. He was a proud one, this *Pura Raza*. The insult of being ridden by an Iber who had until recently been an infantryman had been a calculated move on the part of El Miedo, and Pego's pure blood must be boiling. There was no knowing what he would do to restore his wounded pride.

They were coming closer and closer to where Arriero was poised on top of the hill. The sun was rising behind him, and to El Miedo, the figure of the stallion was like a vision dipped in gold.

Estrella felt the twitch on her nose tighten. She jittered nervously in an odd step, jouncing the lieutenant who sat astride her and causing him to curse incessantly. The harder he dug the sharp spurs into her flanks, the worse he bounced in the saddle.

As the horses around him drew closer, Tijo felt the mare Abelinda's flanks pressing against his leg. She had squeezed in still closer to him.

"You speak horse, boy?"

"Yes." He made a soft nicker indistinguishable from that of a horse.

"This Iber who rides me carries a scabbard with a short

blade just beneath his stirrup strap of the leg that is pressing against you now. You must grab it."

"But how can I get it without him knowing?"

"I'll start a little disturbance. You make it into a big one. Be quick. With the blade, you can cut the rope that tethers you and the twitch line on Estrella's muzzle."

"We can do it," Estrella nickered. "We can, Tijo!"

"But what about the Iber riding you?"

"Once you cut the twitch line, I can throw him easily. He's hardly been able to stay on me as it is."

"I ask for just one thing," Abelinda said.

"What's that?" Tijo asked.

"If you can break to my side, just over on the outer edge of the *falange* is a small mule and an older one in the jerkline. Try and cut them loose."

"We'll try," Estrella nickered, tossing her head.

A shiver ran through the herd of animals. They had seen Jacinto charge the Ibers. During the tumult in the corral, the notion of being free of these terrible humans had spread. The mules were particularly excited. *Unyoked!* They kept repeating the word almost as if they were polishing it like a precious stone and indeed the notion of freedom began to burn fiercely in their minds like radiant gems, as bright as gold.

Abelinda began a skittish little quickstep, almost like a *paso fino*. "¡Calma! Calma!" her rider said.

"What's the trouble?" asked another rider.

"Ah, the mare does not like the *compacto*."

"Not accustomed to the *falange apretado*. She's just an old plug. Never been in combat." Jacinto glanced at Abelinda. *This will ignite the fire.* Then the mule saw a spurt of blood from where the spurs dug into Abelinda's flanks.

She reared up and whinnied shrilly. *Now, Horse Boy! Now!* With one swift movement, Tijo leaned over and grabbed the blade, pulling it from the scabbard, then he slid from his horse onto Estrella . . . He cut the rope around his waist and slashed at the cord of the muzzle twitch on Estrella. Pandemonium broke loose as a score of horses, forty or more, reared. The lock was broken. Riders fell to the ground. The muskets were fired, setting off more panic, but luckily the shots exploded into the air.

El Miedo was shouting orders, but his voice was lost in the din of shrieking horses and the shouts of Ibers.

"There's the little mule!" Estrella said. "We must cut her loose." Estrella was unsure how they might help the rest of the mules, as there were at least two other jerklines and to cut them free of their yokes with the single blade that Tijo held seemed impossible. But in the panic, mules had begun to rear and carts were toppling over.

Estrella with Tijo were on a straight line now, clear of the fray and heading for Mikki. The mare Abelinda was right beside them. However, she skidded to a halt when she saw El Miedo staggering toward them. The fury radiated off of him like heat from a fire. He was carrying not one but two muskets and was pointing them right at Tijo and Estrella.

"No!" Abelinda shrieked. There was a streak as a dark horse bolted between El Miedo and Estrella. Blood splattered the air. But it was not Abelinda's blood, nor was it Mikki's. Pego! A curtain of flesh hung from his chest. Blood poured onto the ground.

"Go!" he whinnied. "Go!" His eyes rolled back in his head, and then he collapsed.

PART 3

The Mighties

CHAPTER 15

Cut Free

There were close to one hundred horses in all. They kicked up an enormous dust storm in their wake. The new horses who had never before run wild felt something igniting in them, a kindling that was building to a flame — a fire of freedom. They were galloping faster than they ever had before, their hearts uproarious with this newfound liberty. Iron shoes were cast as they ran. Saddles slipped to the horses' sides, and many eventually were shed completely. Their bridles hung half off with the reins trailing. Every time a shoe was cast, a saddle flung to the ground, they whinnied with delight. Never again would they be owned. Never again would they be beaten. Never again would they be the vehicles for the Ibers' greed. The horses pounded across this new land so fast, their hooves devouring the ground. Their veins tingled with the fever of freedom.

They stopped to rest in a strange basin where steam rose from vents and twined up through the air. When the hot vapors first erupted, there was a hissing, then feathery white plumes surged toward the sky. The plumes would linger, then the wind would thin them out until the remnants looked like the filaments of a giant spiderweb stretched across the night. The horses, sweating and breathing heavily, looked about in wonder at this seemingly magical place.

Hold On trotted up to Estrella with Tijo astride. "I can't believe it. You're here! You both escaped," he whinnied joyfully. Tijo reached over and pressed his cheek against the old stallion's face. Hold On felt a wetness. *So these are tears*, he thought. Horses could not shed tears, not tears that came from the deepest of feelings. For a moment, he wished he could cry, to express the overwhelming surge of emotion in his heart.

He ran his muzzle down Tijo's legs toward Estrella's flanks and bristled. The smell of the leather saddle nauseated him.

"Don't worry," Tijo said, slipping from her back. "I'll take off her saddle and bridle."

He loosened the girth and cast the saddle on the ground. Then he took the bridle from her head and threw it as far as he could.

Estrella gave herself a hard shake to dispel any trace of the foul-tasting metal. Then she looked about, taking in the incredible scene before her.

"There are so many of us now," she said softly, her voice a mix of wonder and apprehension. These newly freed horses did not know what it meant to be wild. Someone would have to teach them, to guide them. But could she be that leader? The last time the herd had turned to her, she'd let them down.

She was also haunted by the image of the fallen Pego, which she couldn't shake from her mind. A welter of confusing emotions swirled within her. She had felt only contempt for the dark stallion for as long she could remember. Had he purposely charged out to take the muskets' fire? Had he truly sacrificed his own life? Why now? What had changed him? She saw the blood spurting from his chest. There'd been an intriguing light in his eyes as he fell dying. It was not the sheen of pride she had seen so many times in his eyes. Not fear. But an odd sort of relief. And perhaps even gladness — gladness to have met death. It was as if he were saying, *I am done but you must live.* It was, she realized, a moment that Pego the proud *Pura Raza* had never before experienced. It was his moment of grace.

"We are free," said a small voice. It was the mare Abelinda. She was shaking her head in wonder, for she no longer wore a bridle. She craned her head around to look at her tawny coat rimed with sweat and blinked in joyous disbelief. "I'm naked!

No saddle! No bridle and just one iron shoe left!" She bucked ecstatically.

"But I still have my yoke even though I am not in the jerk-line." Mikki tipped her head this way and that.

"I'll fix that," Tijo said. He still had in his hand the blade that he had taken from the Iber. He began sawing at the strap beneath Mikki's neck.

Yazz trotted over and gave Tijo an affectionate nudge with her long nose.

"Who are you?" Mikki looked at the grizzled mule.

"Another mule. Once in the yoke like you. But I left before you were born."

"I remember you well," Abelinda said. "I couldn't quite understand why you had left." She shook her head. "But, yes, I do believe you sowed the first seeds that night and now look at us." She looked toward Jacinto and remembered his words. "Freedom is not given. It's taken. And then Jacinto showed us the way. We took our freedom. Seized it!"

Mikki was tossing her head with delight and had begun to romp around in the swirls of steam. She bucked, reared, then bucked again. "I love it! I just love it!" She whinnied wildly into the air. The sound of her sheer delight spun up into the frothy white of the steam plumes. It was a fine sound, a glorious sound that came from someplace deep within her and spiraled up and up in rings of pure happiness.

Meanwhile, Tijo had moved on to a nearby colt and was cutting away its bridle. Then he went to another horse and freed that one of its saddle. He was very solemn as he performed these tasks. It was like a beautiful ritual. He cut the straps with a quiet dignity. But the sound that Tijo loved the most was when he would drop the metal bit onto the ground. Usually, there was a dull thud, but if the bit hit a rock, there was a satisfying clink. He pried off what horses' shoes he could. Some, however, held fast, and they would have to wait for the wear and tear of the trail before they would be loose enough to cast.

He worked all night, and when the morning light broke, the shadows of the Mighties crept across the basin. They were nearer then they had thought. It was less than a half day of travel to the base of the mountain range and then straight up, or so it seemed. But brimming with the exhilaration of their new freedom, these horses and mules were ready. Anything was better than the bit and bridle, the yoke and the spurs. "I thought I would die in a jerkline," said one old mule, shaking his head in wonder.

"You know," said another, "in a jerkline with a yoke, you can never look up. You never see the blue of the day sky or the stars of the night. I feel I've become part of not simply a new land but a new universe."

Estrella felt a growing anxiety. She was free. The twitch was gone from her muzzle, the saddle from her back, and the disgusting taste of metal — gone, but would she ever forget it?

Now that the initial thrill was wearing off, the newly freed horses and mules were starting to grow nervous. They'd never lived without human masters, and didn't know what to do.

"Hold On," she whispered. "Must we teach them to be free?"

"Freedom can't be taught. Remember, most of them still wear the shoes nailed into their hooves. It takes a while. Freedom might be seized as the mule, the one they call Jacinto, says, but wildness — well, that is a sensation that is waiting to be revealed. When we cross the Mighties, they will begin to discover it."

"Are we taking them with us?" Estrella asked.

"Why, of course," Hold On said, giving her a stern look. "You will lead them. You are our leader. They are part of the first herd now."

"But, Hold On, there are so many. I . . . I fear . . ."

"Fear what?"

"The Mighties — leading this huge herd now across these mountains to . . . to . . . where exactly? I just have a feeling about the sweet grass, but what if . . ."

"Don't you see, Estrella, that it is your mission to lead these horses and mules to their new lives. You have the vision."

But do I? Estrella thought. She had made a terrible mistake in ignoring the *omo* owl's warning to split the herd. She had been impatient, too eager, and risked the lives of the first herd.

Where was the tiny horse? The sparkling creature had appeared so suddenly in the stall, hovering over that lump of fool's gold. It had turned its head toward her and seemed about to speak. *Fear not . . . fear not*, it had seemed to say. But now she was afraid. Free but frightened. Where was the tiny horse and where was Hope? Hope, who Tijo said carried the spirit of Haru? She needed them now. She had to lead, but who might guide her? In the midst of one hundred horses, she had never felt so alone.

Then suddenly the old scent began to thread through her nostrils, through the remnants of pain from the horrid twitch. It was the sweet grass. She had caught that scent again. It overpowered the smell of the leather saddles still on the horses' backs. It vanquished the taste of the metal. This was their destiny, and it lay on the other side of the Mighties. It was as Hold On had told her — she was the one who must lead them across this mountain range.

"Tijo," she said, "we can't go on until every saddle, every bridle, yoke, and bit has been cut. Only then will they begin to know freedom." She glanced at some mules standing nearby with yokes askew on their shoulders. "Unyoke the mules!"

The lodge of Hope was growing fragile. Without it, Haru was a feeble spirit and completely powerless for her earthly work, which she knew was not finished. She did not precisely understand the creature called the tiny horse. It appeared to fade in and out like the stars. The one thing that Haru did know was that despite the feebleness of her spirit, she must not linger over the field strewn with the bodies of Ibers — many of which had been trampled when the horses and mules escaped.

Haru did not like to see death but was glad that, in the chaos of the stampede, the Chitzen slaves had been able to escape. No creature should be kept in chains, two-legged or four.

Because of her weakened state, Haru had to rely on the winds to carry her spirit in search of her next lodge, if indeed she could find one. But this morning was nearly windless. She must give the faithful coyote, Hope, a chance to restore himself. What a valiant creature he had been!

As the earth warmed, the air would rise, and the first breezes would stir. *Patience, Spirit. Patience,* she counseled herself. *I have nothing to live for, only to die for.* Now, as the heat thickened, the first true breeze of the morning roused itself.

Hope had never in his short life been so exhausted. He curled up not far from the dead body of Pego and the body of an Iber lieutenant who had been trampled to death in the rebellious tumult of the horses. Hardly an ideal place to sleep, but he was desperate. Sleep was what he craved, what he thirsted for. Only sleep could slake him.

What Hope did not realize was that it was not he who was tired, but it was the spirit lodge wearing thin. When Haru found a new lodge, he would revive. But he had been too tired to keep up with the thundering herd of animals. Hope felt a wind stir his fur. *I am haunted by winds,* he thought as the spirit of Haru left him.

When he awoke, it was long past midday. He felt refreshed but lonely. He blinked as he saw a vulture pecking on the remains of Pego. Another vulture lighted down nearby and was examining the body of a dead human. The vulture looked up.

"Hah!" he cawed roughly. "I knew I was right."

"Right about what?" Hope said.

"You weren't dead after all." He twisted his head and looked directly at the other vulture, who raised his bloody beak.

"I just felt that the coyote was more your size," the other vulture replied.

"You didn't want to share. That was the problem."

"Share what? Who was more your size?" Hope asked.

"You," the vulture said, spitting out a metal button from the jacket of the Iber lieutenant. "The problem with humans is their clothes. It takes forever to get a decent bite."

"Well, I'm not human and I'm not dead," Hope said, inching away.

"Yes, that's a problem, too," said the first vulture.

"Let us know when you are!" the other vulture cackled from where he was perched on Pego's rib cage. "Since you don't wear clothes, it'll be a lot less work for us!" Both vultures were cackling madly now.

Hope could not get away fast enough. He felt strong again, without a trace of the exhaustion that had overwhelmed him earlier, but he also felt terribly lonely. He scurried around bodies of Ibers, bodies that had been thrown by horses, then crushed by their stampeding hooves. He needed to find the first herd. He needed decent creatures. Grace, where was Grace? Oh, what he wouldn't give to see Grace again!

CHAPTER 16

Tenyak

Estrella, Hold On, and Arriero stood together surveying the tack and tackle, the tools of restraint that the Ibers had used to shackle the horses and the mules to their will. The other horses were cantering about, jumping, rearing, bucking, wallowing in the ecstasy of their freedom.

"*Es un milagro*," Corazón said softly, trotting up to them. "Look at all this — the bit, the bridles, and you see that stallion over there? He just kicked off the last of his shoes."

"*Milagro*, miracle, is not quite the right word," Hold On said thoughtfully. "No. It's more a sign of will — what free will can do. That stallion kicked off his shoes because he was determined. He did not even wait for Tijo to come with his blade and pry them off."

Estrella was listening carefully. "And I believe it was free will that made Pego die for us. He charged out between us and the two muskets that El Miedo fired." She paused for a long time and looked at the horses milling about in the long shadows of the Mighties.

"I think," she began again slowly, "I know what we need to do first. We are many now. To cross these mountains with so many is no easy task. I think we must first send scouts to seek out the best trails. I want us to keep together, but there might be times when we must separate. We need three scouts who can find good trails with good forage. Sometimes a trail might be able to support all of us. But the grazing will grow thin. There will not be enough for all of us all the time on a single trail."

"Estrella is right." The mare Abelinda had come up to the small gathering. "When we started with El Miedo, we numbered six hundred in all. When we would pass through even good pasture, there was not enough to nourish but half that number. It became worse and worse. Fights broke out. But we were in the flatlands, the plains." Abelinda tipped her head up. The jagged snowcapped peaks of the Mighties clawed at the sky. "There cannot be much that grows up there," she whispered.

The solemnity of this moment was crushing. No one spoke for a long time. Estrella longed for just a glimmer of the tiny horse, and Tijo was lost in thoughts of Haru. Had she worn out the spirit lodge of Hope? Would she find another?

Estrella gave herself a shake and twitched from her withers down through the large muscles of her shoulders. She had to stop looking for this glimmer. The tiny horse would come when it would come. One could not summon the elusive creature.

"Abelinda, would you serve as a scout? You know how much grazing can support this number of horses."

The mare nodded. "I would be honored." Even though Abelinda had shed her shoes, she still possessed an Old Land manner about her. Estrella could see that Angela and Corazón approved of her.

Now Sky came up. "I would like to be a scout."

"But you are so young," Estrella replied doubtfully.

He tossed his head in indignation. "Estrella, I am older than you! Remember, you were foaled at sea during the voyage, where I was foaled a month before on land on First Island."

"That's true," Estrella said with a sigh. Being the leader of the herd had been a great honor, but it had also made her feel old beyond her years.

"My legs are strong. And you know I have a good muzzle on me. I pick up scents others don't." He paused and then added quickly, "Except for Hold On, of course."

Estella nodded. Sky was eager and energetic, and would do his very best to serve the herd. "Then you are a scout."

Abelinda spoke up. "I think we need one more scout. A big strong horse." All heads swung toward Arriero.

"Of course," Arriero replied. "I, too, am honored."

A memory loomed up with fierce intensity in Estrella's mind. That first year in the New Land they had been tracked by two big mountain cats for the better part of a day. When the cats broke into a run and began their chase in earnest, the four stallions — Arriero, Bobtail, Grullo, and Hold On — worked together to wear them out and draw them near through a series of quick dodges and feints. Then Arriero, the largest and most powerful, had spun around just as the male was about to attack and bucked. He had caught him with his hind hooves, ripping open his belly, and flung him into the air. Yes, they needed Arriero as a scout. He was powerful and lithe. A monster when he set his mind to it. They were after all going into a territory very different from any they had experienced.

It was not simply high country. It was an immense mountain range. Thick with trees they had never seen, animals they might not have ever imagined. A chill breeze swept down from the mountains. Within minutes, the air turned silver in a slanting wind full of sleet and ice. Winter had come.

An eagle flew over the crown of the fir trees that moaned in the wind. Her gizzard flinched slightly, and then a warm riffle of a breeze stirred her primary feathers. *I am flying into the cold Taku winds. So why is there this warm current?* Then it dawned on her. *By my talons! A spirit has lodged in me.* She had heard of such things, but she had never quite believed it, and even if she had, she could not believe that a spirit would choose her. Was this a compliment? She immediately chastised herself for having such a thought. It was vain. Eagles had to be careful about that. Her mum had constantly warned her about vanity. "Vanity is treacherous. Vanity is only for fools."

Enough! a voice resonated in her. Yet it was not quite a voice. The eagle was confused.

You are not vain. Now we have work to do.

The eagle teetered as if she had hit a rough patch of air.

Work . . . I'm all for work. There's a good trout stream two points off my port wing. And I'm a great fisher bird. I can get some lovely fish.

Spirits don't need food.

The eagle was not sure exactly what the spirit meant but decided not to ask. Instead, she felt a strong urge to introduce herself. *My name is Tenyak.* Haru was taken off guard. She had never had a lodge creature introduce itself. Nor had she met one so talkative.

What's yours?

My name is Haru. The human you see below on that horse is my boy, Tijo. He has a strange and wonderful understanding of these creatures. The horse he rides is Estrella, a young filly. She is the leader of the first herd. This country the Ibers call the New

Land, but for the horses, it is the Old Land. They are returning, and it is our work to make sure they get to where they are
meant to be.

Tenyak knew exactly where they were meant to be — the
Valley of the Dawn on the other side of the Mighties, where
the grass grew thick and tall and its nodding flower heads
looked in the dawn light almost blue. Where winter came late,
and summers lingered.

What is that I see twinkling ahead where the sun just set?

Aaah! Haru sighed happily. She knew she had picked the
right lodge for her spirit. *It is another spirit, you see. It is the spirit
of the dawn horse. It, too, will help with our work. But the dawn
horse is a shy creature. Bashful, a bit timid.*

Just one moment, Haru continued. She felt Tenyak's wings
angle as the eagle began to carve a turn. *First, I must ask of you
one thing. There is something that must be retrieved, brought back
to its rightful owner.*

Yes? Tenyak said. *What is it?*

*A blanket — a blanket made from the hide of a white
buffalo.*

A white buffalo! Tenyak nearly staggered in flight. *I thought
they were creatures of legends. Not real.*

*All legends start from something real. But this one was real, I
assure you. The blanket made from its pelt was stolen. Stolen by
the Chitzen chieftain, who is now a captive of the Ibers.*

And then, perhaps because Tenyak's being was so suffused with the spirit of Haru, the eagle knew instantly.

And this blanket belongs to the one they call Horse Boy?

Indeed, Haru replied, and felt the eagle once more tip her wings and begin a banking turn toward the encampment of the Ibers.

CHAPTER 17

A Blanket Returned

Even after the chieftain and the rest of his clan escaped, he continued to be haunted by terrible dreams. This one was different, though. He was dreaming of being free and powerful again. He was riding the dark stallion once more. The Burnt River People were again fearful, respectful. He was no one's slave but everyone's master. A sharp snort suddenly awakened him. When he opened his eyes, he saw a gleeful light dancing in his wife Pinyot's eyes. *What is she so cheerful about?* He growled at her, and she laughed. He was about to leap to his feet, but something knocked him over. His eyes widened in disbelief. An immense eagle stood on his chest. She raised one talon and raked the space just in front of his eyes. The message was clear. The eagle would rip out his eyes *if . . . if . . .*

if what? It was clear that the eagle was demanding something of him.

"If what?" he blurted out. And at that moment Pinyot laughed.

"If you don't give up the blanket!"

"But what does an eagle want with a blanket?" He felt the talons digging into his chest.

"I told you the blanket was cursed. It was Haru's and therefore Tijo's," Pinyot whispered in a scalding voice.

The eagle drew her face close to the chieftain's, and deep in the amber of the eagle's eyes, the chieftain saw the face of Haru peering back. In that instant, the chieftain fell over dead and rolled off the blanket.

Pinyot stood up. She glanced at this man who had beaten her so mercilessly for so long, then began to fold the blanket into a neat bundle. She pulled some twine from the fastenings of her moccasins and tied it around the bundle.

"There!" she said softly.

The eagle nodded. The small nod was more acknowledgment than she had ever received from her husband. She felt her eyes start to fill. Then, grasping the bundle, the eagle spread her wings and flew out from the shelter. Pinyot stepped through the opening and watched until the eagle's wings faded into the night, but she could still see the white of the blanket.

She now caught her breath. *How could this be? How could I*

have just walked from that shelter? She was walking quickly now, and no one seemed to notice. Pinyot kept walking. She walked right out of the encampment. She chuckled to herself. *Perhaps I have become a spirit, too — an* omo. But in that moment, she winced. A sharp rock poked at the sole of her moccasin. And it felt good. She was not a spirit. She was not dead. She was alive. She was free. So she kept on walking into the night.

CHAPTER 18

The Beaver Pond

"I'm going to break off all my teeth at this rate," Verdad muttered. He had thought this trail would lead to some promising forage. But such was not the case. The only vegetation they could find was the mosses and lichen on rocks, which, although tasty, were never sufficient. They had made fairly good progress, more than halfway to the top of the ridgeline. But the weather in the Mighties was fretful, alternating between blasts of warm sunshine and, two minutes later, thick clouds rolling in with sleet or snow. The snow so far had not been heavy, for which they were thankful, as some of the inclines were quite steep and to attempt them in snow would have been difficult.

"You can stop complaining," Sky snorted, trotting up to Verdad. Sky was the scout for Verdad's group, which was the smallest one of the now immense herd, with only twenty horses.

"What, you found something? Real grass?"

"There's a beaver pond not far from here — cattails, berries."

"No prickles?" Verdad asked.

"My, aren't we getting picky about prickles! Verdad, might I remind you that we have been in desert country for most of our time here and the plants there had nothing but prickles for the most part."

Verdad ignored the criticism. "Where is this pond?"

Sky looked at the sun. In the short time since they had divided into separate groups, each with its own scout, the shadows of the evening had started to settle earlier and earlier. Winter was fast closing in on them. The sun was halfway down. "By twilight, I think we should get there."

"That's not long."

"Not at all. Now round up our herd and come along."

"Is there enough for everyone?"

"There is enough for all four herds. I've already told Estrella, Abelinda, and Arriero."

"Enough for all?"

"Yes, all!"

Verdad was delighted. Although they had been traveling for a few days, it had seemed like forever. He yearned for his mates.

He liked these other horses and mules fine, but his heart was really with the first herd. Verdad had never known his dam or his sire. If he had any blood siblings, he did not know them. The first herd was all these things to him — dam, sire, and siblings.

He whinnied the signal to move on. "We're going to join up with the first herd again. All of us!"

"Oh, bless my withers," Angela said. "I know it's only been a few days, but I miss them all so much: Bella, Grullo — known him since I was a filly — and dear Hold On. Ah! Hold On. To see that old gray stallion."

Corazón, who was nearby, looked up and sighed when Angela said Hold On's name. That wonderful wise stallion with his dapple gray coat and his poor old eyes that had turned milky in blindness. How she missed him.

"And we won't have to be eating rocks for a while," Angela said. "I mean this moss is not bad-tasting, but I'd give my fetlock just to have a plant that grows straight out of the earth and not on a rock."

The horses started on their way, following Sky toward the beaver pond. They had not gone far when the colt overheard the two old mares talking softly.

"Angela," Corazón said. "Is there something wrong with your leg? Your walk seems a bit off."

"Oh, I think I just have a small rock caught in my frog. That's all." Angela was quiet for a while. "Don't you think it strange, Corazón, that those little creatures that live in ponds are called frogs? Why would they call such a creature, a little old slimy thing that hops about on those spindly legs and has those bulgy eyes, after the bottom of a horse's hoof? It doesn't make sense, does it?"

"There are a lot of things that don't make sense, Angela," Corazón said. "Bits and bridles don't make sense. Muskets don't make sense."

"Well, that, of course, is just plumb crazy. But naming those slime hoppers *frogs* makes no sense, either."

"What made you even think of this?"

"We're going to a pond, a beaver pond. We might see a few frogs as well as beavers. I guess that's why."

Sky enjoyed listening in on the two old mares' conversation. How often had he heard them chattering away about some ridiculous little thing. Their voices made the world, this new land, a cozier place. But he was concerned about Angela's hoof. If this beaver pond proved as good as it looked for grazing, he would suggest to Estrella that they wait there for a few days to give the old mare's hoof a rest.

The sun had just set, casting a violet tint on the water when they arrived. The edges of the pond were fringed with cattails and tall grasses. Small clusters of horses were scattered about, grazing happily. Sky and his horses were the last to arrive.

Estrella came cantering up with Tijo on her back. "This is a good place. I think by morning it might be snowing. So start grazing."

"What about you, Tijo? Anything for you to eat?" Hold On asked.

"I found a grouse and caught two frogs and roasted them."

"Speaking of frogs," Sky said. "Angela has a rock caught in hers. Could you get it out, Tijo?"

"I thought her trot was off when I saw her coming," Estrella said.

"I heard it was off!" Hold On added, flicking his ears.

"Let me have a look," Tijo said as he slipped off Estrella and went over to Angela.

Estrella looked at him as he picked up the old mare's hoof and, bracing it between his knees, bent over to examine it. The boy had grown not just taller, but his back had broadened. His shoulders had heft and muscle. She looked at the other horses from the first herd who had gathered around to watch Tijo as he picked out the small rock with his bone knife. *He's becoming a man*, Estrella thought.

And she and the two colts were changing as well. Soon, she would no longer be called a filly but a mare, and Sky and Verdad would no longer be colts but stallions. An odd thought crossed Estrella's mind, making her suddenly wistful. *I wish my dam, Perlina, could see me as a mare.*

Tijo looked up at Sky. "The hoof doesn't look good," he said softly.

"It doesn't smell good, either, Angela. I hope you don't have green hoof," Hold On said, his eyes full of concern.

"Nonsense." The old mare snorted.

Sky cocked his head to one side to draw Estrella's attention and walked a few paces away from Angela. She trotted over to him.

"What is it, Sky?" Estrella asked. She looked directly into his eyes, which always had fascinated her. With one blue eye and one black, it was like looking into day and night at the same time. She could see, however, that the blue one, usually as bright as a clear morning sky, was shadowed with worry.

"Angela won't let on how much that hoof is troubling her. I think if it's possible we should wait here a few days. The grazing seems good."

"Of course, a few days' rest might help her," Estrella replied.

They both looked over at Angela as she limped toward the pond to graze on the cattails near a group of mules.

"Why doesn't the little mule Mikki graze? She seems to be hanging back," Sky said.

"Oh, I think the water frightens her. Remember the crocodiles when we first got to that beach far to the south?

And they had them on First Island, too. Maybe she spent time on First Island or heard the others talk about them," Estrella said.

"Don't worry. I'll go down and help her. She needs to graze." Sky turned and headed for the little mule.

Hold On had now come up. Estrella's gaze lingered on Sky as he went to help the little mule.

"Worried about Angela?" Hold On said.

"Yes, a bit. Sky thinks we should stay here a few days. Give that hoof time to heal. I agree. In the meantime, I think I, and a couple of the scouts, can go out and find good trails. And *hallums*."

"*Hallums?*" Hold On flicked his ears.

Estrella was not sure where the word had come from. Possibly in a dream that she couldn't recall. But she had awakened with this notion of *hallums*, the best routes through the treacherous Mighties. When she'd awoken that morning, she saw an immense eagle floating over a mountain peak. The eagle, she was sure, had been in the dream, too.

Tijo's first words to her upon wakening that morning after the dream were "You saw the eagle."

"And did you?" she asked.

He had nodded solemnly.

"Haru!" Estrella nickered softly. An eagle with the spirit of Haru. Now the dream she had had made sense. Haru would spy the *hallums*. The best routes were not necessarily the short-est in distance, but they were less steep and far less dangerous, especially if there was ice on the trail.

A full moon had begun to rise painting the beaver pond silver. The beavers' water trails sparkled in the night as they plied their way silently across the pond with the branches of cottonwood, alder, and willow that they had gnawed down. They did not seem to mind the horses grazing on the sedges and cattails. One had even told Hold On that they considered the soft plants unappetizing although very nourishing. They did not talk much as their mouths were always gripping the branches they had just gnawed.

Hold On caught the scent first. A tremor of excitement ran through him from his withers to his tailbone. "It's him!"

"Who?" asked Estrella.

"It's . . . it's . . ." Hold On was so excited he could hardly get out the name. "It's Hope!"

A cry went up as all the horses began whinnying. And Hope came bounding onto the banks of the pond.

"You're back!" Yazz brayed.

"Yes, I am." Hope trotted out from a thicket. He greeted the horses, but before Estrella could join them, Tijo walked up quietly to Estrella. He needed to talk. She could tell. She didn't even have to lower her head now for him to reach her ear.

"The eagle is near. I can feel it. Let's go now while the moon is still rising. It will soon be full. Good light to see by."

"Yes, you're right." But there was a part of her that wanted to stay. She watched as Sky led the little mule Mikki to the water's edge while giving her a nudge, then nickering words of encouragement. She wanted to watch these new members of her herd learn to become free. She looked back at the horses once more, close to one hundred of them now, grazing around the moon-glazed water. She could not help but think back to the beach where they had swum to shore after being cast into the sea. That was the first time her hooves had ever touched the ground, earth, the New Land. In those days, they did not know what it meant to be owned by humans, but at the same time, they did not know what it mean to be wild. Now they knew. Sky was gently herding the little mule to another clump of sedges. He seemed no longer a colt to her. He was large, almost as big as Arriero. He had grown in other ways, however, and not simply size. As a young colt, he had been impatient and a bit selfish, but over the years, Sky had become tender and caring.

But she knew she had to go with Tijo. Something was calling to him, her fellow long spirit, and they had to follow. Their survival depended upon it.

CHAPTER 19

The Eye in the Sky

"Here," Tijo said. Estrella stopped. Tijo tipped his head back and looked straight up to the top of a towering fir tree.

"What is it?" she asked.

"This is where the eagle nests at the top of this tree. Do you see it?"

Estrella lifted her head. "I see something huge up there. So big it blocks out the stars."

"That's an eagle's nest." Tijo stood up on Estrella's back and reached for the nearest branch.

"You're going to climb all the way up there?"

"Yes," he replied.

Estrella paused, suddenly nervous about Tijo putting himself in danger. Tijo read her thoughts and smiled. "Don't worry.

I'll be back soon." Then, from her back, he swung up onto the branch directly over his head. Soon he had disappeared into the dense web of the tree's branches.

She felt terribly alone. She could hear the creak of the tree and Tijo's breathing as he climbed higher and higher toward the nest and the eagle, the spirit lodge for Haru. But she, Estrella, was left behind with no one. A small breeze stirred around her front hooves. She looked down. There was a swirl of shimmering light, as if a cluster of stars had fallen down from the sky through the branches of the tree. The starry bits began to gather into a form. The memory of her dam flooded through her and with it the scent of the sweet grass.

"Oh!" Estrella gasped.

"You are not alone, Estrella. Never alone!"

It was the tiny horse. And she was speaking. This was the first time Estrella had heard the voice. And it was a female horse. Of this she was certain.

"But why have you come? Why are you speaking to me now? Now at last."

"The farther I am away from humans, the stronger my voice grows. Look up, Estrella. Look up!"

"I see mountain peaks that scrape the stars."

"And what else?"

Estrella blinked. She saw the head of an eagle looking down at her.

"Tenyak is the eagle's name," the tiny horse murmured. "She'll guide you over the *hallums*, Estrella."

Another voice now came whispering down from the tree. Estrella recognized it immediately. It was coming from the eagle, but it was the spirit voice of Haru. *Tenyak is my eye in the sky. We shall guide you to the* hallums, *but between the* hallums, *there are dangers. Remember, even as a spirit I am not all-powerful.*

These were the same chilling words that Haru had spoken when their first attempt to escape the Ibers had failed.

Tijo had not reached the nest yet but heard the voice of the spirit lodge talking throughout his ascent. Now he clambered over the edge of the nest. But he was not quite prepared for what he found. *What is this?* he thought. It seemed to be a snowy cover spread across the nest, but although white, it was not snow. Hardly snow, for it radiated warmth. He felt his heart race. A wonderful stream of sensations flooded through him. Were they memories or feelings? He felt suspended in a space between consciousness and dreaming. Between the time, he was a mere infant safe in Haru's arms and now nearly grown. A space between unknowing and knowing. Between memory and sensation. Between starlight and darkness. The outlines of the world he had known were breaking down imperceptibly, and a deeper, more profound world was revealing itself. He was sifting through a myriad of feelings and memories. He felt the eagle's eyes on him. The eyes of Haru! He reached out and touched the white. "My blanket."

"Yes, your blanket, Tijo. It is yours to keep. You have more than earned it."

Strands of moonlight shuttled through the clouds as Tijo, with the blanket neatly rolled and tied to his back, descended through the branches to where Estrella waited patiently. *I am watched, and I am warm!* he thought happily. With the eyes of the eagle and the warmth of this blanket, they could possibly make it over the Mighties.

Estrella heard Tijo descending the tree. He slipped onto her back.

"What is that you carry?"

"The blanket."

"The blanket that Haru made?"

"Yes, the one the chieftain stole."

"And it is back now." Estrella nickered with delight. "It is yours again."

"It is ours, Estrella."

They heard the beating wings of the eagle Tenyak as she rose in the night, and when Estrella looked down at the tree roots where the tiny horse had first appeared, she saw just a dim flickering and then it melted away like a star in the first gray of a new dawn. Tijo stroked Estrella's shoulder with his hand, and she turned her head around and rubbed his shin with her soft muzzle.

It had begun to snow. The flakes silver and delicate fell slowly and obliquely in the light whisper of wind. The horse and the boy didn't say much on the way back to the pond. Though the tiny horse had vanished, the scent of the sweet grass still flowed through Estrella, and though the eagle circled high into the night, the voice of Haru still threaded through Tijo like a song, not precisely words but more like chimes stirred by a breeze. These memories — the scent and the voice — were the things that would carry them across the Mighties, over the passes between the peaks, and they began to shine like moonlit stones on a dark trail as the snow fell softly.

CHAPTER 20

The River

The jagged peaks of the Mighties had dissolved into the mountain mists. The trees shuddered in the icy winds that tumbled over the crests. The scouts had found three decent trails that twined together into a loose braid as they made their way toward the first pass. Although neither Estrella nor Tijo had spoken of their meeting with the eagle Tenyak, or the reappearance of the tiny horse, the first herd seemed to sense that both had met with their spirit creatures, their guides. And most interestingly, this knowledge appeared to have seeped through the nearly one hundred horses and mules that followed them. Often, the animals tipped their heads up and scanned the sky for the spreading wings of the eagle. However, the thick mist that encircled the peaks made spotting the bird difficult. But when they did, a palpable sense of relief ran like a current through the herd. On a bright day, the bird's broad wingspan printed a comforting shadow on the steep rocky inclines and seemed to almost smooth them down to a flatness similar to the three *hallums* they had already crossed.

The new horses had adapted to freedom quickly, especially the mare Abelinda. She was an interesting horse who was obviously highly regarded by the others. Yazz had commented on her uncanny intelligence, for she had known her when she was part of El Miedo's expedition.

Estrella was sure that it had been Abelinda who had spread this notion of freedom throughout the corral. It was Abelinda who had primed the creatures to be ready to run free when the time came. And it was now Abelinda who had comprehended the notion of the spirit guides and how their own lives were linked to a larger destiny.

The three different strands of the loose braid of horses were making their way up toward the fourth *hallum*. They kept their eyes on the trail but would often scan the sky for the eagle. However, the fog had grown thicker. Despite the steepness of the terrain, the grazing was good, with more than a few winter-berries that the horses had come to love. They actually liked the foliage better than the fruit. Sky had gone back down to check on Angela. Their rest at the beaver pond had helped her some, but he had noticed that on this day with the steep terrain, the mare was moving more slowly.

"I'm fine, I'm fine," she whinnied. "No need to worry. I am just enjoying these berries."

Corazón, who was grazing nearby, flashed a look to Sky that said it all: *Her hoof is worse!*

"Well, it's not far to the next *hallum* and the slope on the other side coming down is not bad. And there's a river."

"Oh, that will be so nice for Tijo. He must be sick of eating berries, and I know the hunting isn't so good. But fish! That boy can catch any fish."

But, thought Sky, *will Angela be able to cross the river? If it's deep enough to swim, that will be good. But if it is shallow and the riverbed is cobbled with rock, the pain on her hoof will be terrible.*

Later that afternoon, the strands of the braids of horses met on the sandy bank of the river to begin their crossing. From the shore, the river appeared placid, with barely a hint of a riffle on its surface. The shadow of the eagle's wings was printed on the smooth green water. A gentle rain began to fall, dimpling the slow-moving flow. The horses were eager to start across. The water felt good on Angela's hoof. The old mare could see that the horses ahead of her had reached a deeper part of the river and were swimming. She would be there soon and knew the deep water would feel even better as she would be weightless. For in truth, the lameness was creeping up her leg. A thread of lightning crackled overhead. The muscles from her fetlock to her knee were hot with pain, but the chill of this water was so soothing. She had reached the deep part now and luxuriated in her weightless state. *This is freedom, too,* she thought. *Freedom from pain, freedom from pretending there is no pain. Freedom from trying to keep up.* She closed her eyes and basked in the delight of not feeling a single twinge.

Suddenly, she realized she had drifted a bit away from the others. The lightning overhead had intensified, as had the wind. It was as if the whole world of the river had changed in a second. Bolts of lightning stabbed the water. A large rock that rose above the surface in a froth of rapids suddenly split apart as a dagger of lightning sliced down from the sky. She felt the deep pull of the river. An undercurrent that she had not been aware of through the scrim of her nearly numb leg was pulling her away. Panic filled her. She tried to swim, but the harder she tried, the stronger the current seemed to become. She looked wildly around her. A view of the others was obliterated in the heavy downpour. It was as if the entire sky were emptying into this swollen and raging river. Seconds later, Angela was swept around a bend. The last horse she saw was Corazón, her eyes wild as she searched for her old friend. Her mouth open and screaming. Screams that could not be heard over the howl of the wind, the roar of thunder. Angela felt the scrape of the riverbed beneath one hoof. If she could only get a purchase, she might be able to drag herself from the mindless surge of the river.

On the shore, a grizzly bear crept from her den. She shook her paw and bellowed her wrath at the sky, cursing the bear god. Her den would be flooded again. "Why? Why?" she howled to the river god. "What kind of god are you? This is not your time. Spring is the time. Twice now you have scoured me from my den."

She waded into the water. Cursing and slapping the waves. She was sick of fish. Fish would not nourish the cubs growing inside her. Last year, her newborns had died because she had no milk. She had no milk because she had no fat. She had no fat because there had been no red meat. And there had been no red meat because . . . because she didn't know. The meat trail had disappeared for some mysterious reason that she could not begin to ponder. But her cubs had died. Died of starvation. She, too, would die of starvation, but the little ones, the cubs, died first. She felt herself growing thinner, weaker each day. Her fur pelt hung like rags from her bones.

She would become prey to huge bears, a female like Unka who always seemed to find prey. Unka, it was rumored, had even eaten her own cubs. She was mad, that bear. There was something wrong with her. She was unlike any other grizzly. She was white to begin with, but not white like the ones from the far north with the webbed paws. The soles of those bears' feet and the inside of their paws were covered with hair. Unka was unlike them and bigger than any grizzly male. *She'll come and get me,* the grizzly thought as she railed at the storm. *What's left for me, a cubless female? The world has no use for my kind. I shall die alone. Unka will find me. I shall be no match for her. My flesh consumed by Unka. My bones left to dry and be bleached by the sun and then most likely be swept away by the rising flood of the river, come spring. And the bones of my cubs? The little fragile bones, what will become of them?*

She took her paw and, looking down, wiped the sleet and hail from the fur of her face and muzzle. When she looked up, she saw something odd staggering from the water. The wind drove a scent toward her. *RED BLOOD! MEAT! My cubs will live!*

The roar was deafening. Angela looked up. Her eyes rolled back in terror. Never had she seen anything so large as the fearsome creature before her. The head was massive. The snout squarish, and below that was the most terrifying mouth imaginable, with fangs as long as a donkey's ears.

It seemed like only moments before, Angela had been relishing the absence of pain when her feet had left the riverbed and she had suspended herself in the lovely cold and numbing water. Then there was the sudden fright as she had been swept away. But now she knew there would be pain again. She hoped the pain would not last long. And she did think that she saw more than selfish hunger in the creature's eyes. Yes, it was desperate but not just for its own sake.

The bear did not rush her. She seemed to sense that Angela had given up. She knew with one swat of her immense paw she could knock the horse down. It wouldn't run. She saw how it stood cautiously on three of its legs. The fourth lifted just above the water's surface. The creature was lame. This would be easy.

The bear lunged. All Angela could think was *Better than the muskets to die this way . . . Yes, better than the muskets is this death, for I am nourishing something. Something that will live.*

The bear looked deep into her eyes and saw something she had never seen before, not savagery but grace. And so the bear thanked Angela as she lay dying. Thanked her for giving her own life so her cubs would be born, and she would have milk and they could feed and not starve like the ones before.

CHAPTER 21

The Law of the Mighties

The storm eventually blew out, and Angela's blood curled away on the eddies of the river. The trout swam out from their havens under the rim of rocks. The bear lumbered off to find a winter den to sleep and sink into her drowsy half-waking dreams of cubs, suckling cubs, and the crisp air bearing the sweet scent of milk.

It took the herd four days to find what was left of Angela. The swollen river had retreated, and the barrel of her rib cage soared up in the shallows not far downstream from where she had died. It was sunrise, and everything seemed luminous; even the white ribs had a radiance and did not look, at first, as if they belonged to anything dead or, for that matter, that had ever been alive.

Corazón knelt down in the water. "This is Angela," she said, her voice heavy with heartache.

The eagle settled on a nearby rock. Tijo and Estrella regarded the bird. It was as if Haru spoke silently in their heads. *I told you I am not all-powerful.* Estrella looked at the glinting play of light dancing on the water.

The scintillations of light as the rising sun hit its surface. The loneliness of this canyon that it cut through. The stones in the river were distorted by the refraction of the light passing through the water. Each stone might have had a story, Estrella thought. Stones were thought not to be alive, and yet it was not as if they had ever died but had rather been worn and polished by time. Trout flashed by. One even circled the shallows where Angela's bones lay.

Corazón was making small whimpering noises as she stood over her friend's skeleton.

"I was the one who named her," the old mare said softly. "You might not know it" — she nodded toward Abelinda, who stood near Mikki and several horses from El Miedo's expedition — "but once her name had been Fea."

"Fea?" a stallion asked. "Fea, you mean *ugly*?"

"Indeed. Because she had those spots on her muzzle. But I called her Angela." She paused, then continued, her voice gathering strength. "I called this because when we were cast overboard by the Seeker we were all terribly frightened. But she kept saying to me that she knew I could do it. She stayed by me when the shark circled. She gave me strength and courage. And so I told her when we landed on that first beach, 'They should call you Angela.' For indeed, she was my angel in the sea." Corazón heaved a bit as if swallowing a deep pain. "I told her that she was more, so much more than the spots on her muzzle."

Corazón felt a twinge deep within that big heart for which Angela had named her. *If only she had not gone lame. If only!* They had shared so much, from their lives in the Old Land to the New Land. They had met as young fillies. Once, when Corazón was sold but the prospective buyer did not like the looks of Angela as he sought a matched pair for his bride, Corazón had said, "Oh, Fea, if only I had spots on my muzzle like you!" Angela said to her, "And then they would call you Fea as well."

"I wouldn't care," Corazón had answered. "If only," she had sighed.

Then her friend replied, "*If onlys* are like failed prayers. So don't waste your time on that, dear."

So Corazón decided that to honor her dearest friend, she'd best not think *if only.* But it did not mean she stopped missing her lifelong friend. It did not mean that there was not a hollow place in her that would never be filled, a lonely canyon in her very soul.

"And she called you Corazón," Estrella said, "because you have a big heart." *Even though it might be broken,* the filly thought. However, Estrella did not say these words but continued to stare at the rib cage. Eventually, she imagined these bones of Angela would be swept away completely. There was a channel on the other side where the river had once run but not now. Something had diverted the water course. How often had that course changed, and how many more times would it change? But eventually, all things would come together. The strands of the river, the bones would break down into sand, the stones would tumble and fracture. All things begin to mingle and weave together. The light, the water, the valleys, the rock that would rise up to make the Mighties. They all flowed through time and merged into one.

Hope had been running with the herd for several days now. He was devastated by the death of Angela. He was frustrated that he could not better serve the herd. A spirit no longer lodged within him, but he felt the need to help the herd. Was there nothing he could do to help them? He was a fraction of a horse's size. There was no way he could have fended off the grizzly, but there must be something he could do. *Perhaps I should stop thinking about providing a lodge for another creature's spirit. Perhaps I should just be more of a coyote — not the trickster, but the tracker.*

The thought bloomed in his mind. Hope already knew that he did not have to be the kind of coyote his father had been, deceitful and angry. He was not that sort of animal. He never could be. But he did have skills that were unique to his kind. His sense of smell was vastly superior to that of any horse. His ears were larger for the size of his head than many animals. The grizzly bear's ears were rather stubby for such big creatures. Hope was little; his very smallness was a boon. The herd had four scouts — Estrella, Sky, Abelinda, and Arriero. All big horses.

But their main task was to scout for good trails with good forage. They might pick up the scent of a predator, but in fact, they were too big, too far from the ground to pick up what Hope could. When they had come upon Angela's body, it was Hope who had picked up the lingering scent of the bear. But more important, he had followed the muddy footprints and found a tree not far from the river where the grizzly had rubbed off the bark, scratching its back. Her back. Hope could tell just from the scent left behind that it was a female.

He had already warned Estrella two days before they crossed the river that something like a mountain cat, but not exactly, had been near, and then he had found its paw prints. Smaller than a mountain cat but definitely stealthier. Hope had been shocked when he found how close the cat had come to the horses led by Abelinda. Why it had not attacked he was unsure. The grizzly, however, was much larger and more dangerous than any mountain cat. Hope realized that they were coming

into territory with larger animals now. There were larger preda-
tors for larger prey. There were big-horned sheep, twice the size
of the deer they had seen earlier on. But these enormous horned
sheep were easy prey for a grizzly if they came down to drink in
a creek or river. Hope began to think that although he might
not have the vision of a spirit, he could use his skills, his earth-
bound gifts as a coyote with keen ears and a good snout to help
this herd.

So Hope set out determined that with his coyote instincts he
would help the herd. Their destiny had become bound with his
own. He was not sure why this was so. But it was. His time on
earth, as with all living things, was limited, and he would not
live to destroy as his father had but live to help. *I am small,*
Hope thought, *but I can do much. I am descended from an ances-
try of deceit, but I can live true. I was wronged by my father, but I
can make right by helping these horses. This will be my honor, my
joy, my destiny.*

Hope had not traveled far before he picked up the scent of
the cat again. Why was it always following Abelinda and little
Mikki the mule? Abelinda was moving slower these days, but she
wasn't lame, as Angela had been. Hope was unsure why she had
begun traveling so slowly. Mikki had veered off from the trail
just a bit. The little donkey had found a patch of the winter-

berries that were so succulent. Their smell was heady. But cutting through that smell was the slightly musty odor of the cat.

It was the eyes Hope saw first — amber eyes shining like river stones in the brush. Hope shrieked, "Run, Mikki!" Within two seconds, Abelinda was at the donkey's side.

"You ruined it!" the cat screeched, and skulked out from the bushes. The close-set eyes now bore into Hope. Four other horses arrived, including Grullo and Bella. "How did you know I was here? I pride myself on stealth. Stealth and ambush. That's my game."

"Scent and tracking, that is my game," Hope barked.

The horses were astonished. Mikki was trembling and pressed herself against Abelinda's flank.

"You prey on the weak and the young. I know your kind," Abelinda whinnied shrilly.

"This is the law of the Mighties, fool!"

Hope knew that the cat was right. This was how creatures survived — the ways of predator and prey. The coyote knew he had to convince this cat that was so different-looking from the mountain cats of the desert that the law in this case must be different. He could not show fear. Though this animal was not nearly the size of a grizzly, nor was he as big as a desert mountain cat, he was accustomed to being feared. Hope, trembling, took a step closer. The slits in the cat's amber eyes flashed as if he were surprised.

"Have you ever seen creatures like these before?" Hope cocked his head toward the horses.

"Never, but the flesh smells good," the cat replied.

The horses remained quiet even as the cat seemed to drool at the very thought of their blood.

"And," Hope said, "we have never seen a cat quite like you. The ones from the high desert are larger."

"We're fiercer."

"Oh, I could tell that immediately — and smarter."

The cat seemed pleased with the coyote's words. "So why should I spare these animals?"

"That is a very good question. Not easily answered." Hope was stalling for time and trying to think of an answer. "Well, these creatures that stand before you are called horses. Do you realize they are the first horses in this land?"

"Really, now?" The cat seemed interested.

It was of course not quite true, for there was the tiny horse. *Maybe,* Hope thought, *I should say that. Just be honest.*

"Well, it is not quite accurate . . . Once a long time ago, before even your kind was here, before the Mighties were so mighty, the ancestors of these horses roamed this country."

"Where did they go?"

"No idea," Hope said. "But I am just asking you to let this herd pass now."

"But why? The law of the Mighties is — "

"I know the law of the Mighties. I am asking you to respect the spirit of the Mighties. These horses are coming home. Kindly let them pass."

"And what will I get in return?"

"I make no promises," Hope said humbly.

The cat blinked. He shook his head as if not believing what he heard and saw. He was an animal of action, of supreme slyness and secrecy. And standing before him was this little coyote without a trace of any of those traits. He felt as if he were being crushed by truth, by honesty. Suddenly, the cat felt weak and retreated.

CHAPTER 22

The Place of Firsts

Estrella had lost count of how many *hallums* they had crossed over. But this one by far was the highest. For three days, the horses had followed a steeply sloping face, but finally, they could see a gap in the mountains ahead. It was a bright, sunny day and the shadow of Tenyak's wing slashed the ridgeline.

"You feel it, don't you?" Estrella asked. Hold On, who was carrying Tijo, turned his head toward the filly.

There was no need to ask what she was referring to. Both Tijo and the stallion could tell when Estrella was perceiving visions of the tiny horse.

"All the horses, even the new ones from the corrals of El Miedo, began nickering softly, for they, too, were seeing the flashes of the tiny sprinting figure. *We are coming close to something*, Estrella said. The scent of the sweet grass grew stronger. And that scent along with the fragmented visions of the tiny horse was being shared. The horses picked up their pace despite the steepness.

They were far above the tree line and a bitter wind scoured the *hallum*. A silence had fallen on the horses and mules. There was a rasping sound as the wind churned through the wiry twigs of the scrub bushes.

The creature himself went unnoticed for several minutes. Even Hope had not detected his scent although they had encountered many big-horned sheep. The sheep stood like an immense rock and seemed to blend in perfectly with the boulder behind him. The herd stopped. He appeared immovable, and although he was not blocking their way or making any aggressive gestures, Estrella felt compelled to speak.

"May we pass your way?"

"This is a pass. My way? Perhaps."

Arriero was nervous. He recalled in the old country that there were brigands who preyed on the Ibers, demanding money or silver or gold. *Stand and deliver*, they would say. The words came back to him.

"We have no money, or silver, or gold, sir."

"I want no money, no silver or gold. Such things are worthless," said the creature in a low but gruff voice.

"What do you want?"

"Respect."

The herd was bewildered. "But who are you?" asked Hold On. "We do not even know your name to offer our respect."

"Buck." He was an odd-looking animal. He had a noble bearing and wore his immense, curling horns like a crown. "You are entering a sacred place."

"A sacred place?" Corazón asked, imagining one of the great churches in the Old Land.

"Hallowed," he replied.

"*Hallum?*" Estrella asked.

"If a *hallum* is a passage from one place to another, an in-between place, there must be a place where it all begins and this is that place. The Place of Firsts."

He stepped away from the rock. The horses could now see that the overhang of the rock sheltered a shallow den. Hope caught his breath. There was a slight mound with some very small bones arranged carefully on top. Scattered in and around the bones were beautiful petals, some pink and some a pale lavender. "I'll see you when the *Aurora salix* blooms." The words came back to Hope. Every guard hair on his body bristled. His eyes opened wide. How could flowers bloom on this cold and desolate *hallum?* There was barely enough soil for the tough earth-clinging plants, and all of these had been stripped of their foliage. Was Grace near? Where had these blossoms come from?

At that moment, the figure of the tiny horse glittered in the sun, and the first herd knew that they were most certainly in a hallowed place. They lowered their heads, and many began to swing them from side to side and then stretch their necks. Slowly they put one foreleg far in front of the other, which began to bend at the knee joint, and they sank down until their muzzles touched the ground. Estrella felt a breeze stir her forelock. The star on her brow, for which she had been named, seemed to tingle. The voice of her dam came back to her so clearly: "I shall name you Estrella. I am naming you for all things bright and luminous in the world."

High above, the eagle circled. And the voice of Haru spiraled down. Tijo heard it first. "These are good creatures all. Good creatures now woven together in time." A feeling coursed through Haru that she had often had sitting at her loom when she had almost completed a weaving. The shuttle with the threads would pass through the warp and the weft only a few more times before the rug or the blanket was finished. Haru was not tired, not now. The lodge had not worn thin, but the weaving was nearly complete. She had in her spirit life been the shuttle between the warp and the weft of the living and the dead. It would soon be time for her to return to the spirit camps for good. For the cloth would be finished.

Tenyak swooped down close to the sheep Buck. A big-horned sheep like Buck had also been a lodge for another spirit in another time. That of First Girl. The river that cut through, the earth that had lifted to create the Mighties. They were all now part of that fabric woven by time and inscribed in rock.

CHAPTER 23

Old Dreams

How could flowers be blooming in this cold? Hope kept asking himself. The wind was enough to blow the fur off his back. However, gradually, as the herd made its way down the other side of the *hallum,* the coyote noticed that there was a thread of warm current embedded in the stiff breezes. As they continued their descent, the thread became thicker like a stream. And the overpowering scent of grass filled the air.

Old dreams began to wander through the horses' minds. Dreams that were somewhat familiar but perhaps frayed from time, or it might have been a time before time. The figure of the tiny horse was becoming brighter as the herd slipped away to another day in another world, and the last of the sun's lingering light sprayed pale lavender shadows across the land. The sky became a blue-black dome over their heads, chinked with stars in the crystalline air.

Estrella realized that they were all now sharing the vision of the tiny horse, but soon another figure began to emerge beside it, walking easily on two legs. It was human and small, like a child. She scrambled easily over the rocks. She walked in a companionable silence close to the tiny horse, as if they had known each other for a long time. Her hair fell like the silvery ropes of a waterfall to her shoulders, and surely, Tijo thought, she seemed to be made of mist and vapor rather than flesh and bone. *But of course, she has left her bones behind.* The thought came easily to him and in that moment, she turned and smiled at the coyote. The others soon saw her, too, walking at the side of the tiny horse.

But as these two beings traveled on through the long night, they seemed to grow larger. Soon the girl swung herself up onto the tiny horse, who now was almost as big as Estrella. The night was ending, and the dawn was breaking. The skies appeared bruised with purples and soft pink. There was a thread of gold on the horizon.

The horses were suddenly aware that Abelinda was breathing hard and had slowed. The girl slipped off the tiny horse and walked back to where Abelinda had stopped. She whispered to her and then, patting her softly, urged her forward.

"Not far, not far." It seemed she almost sang the words. There was a lovely rhythm that appeared to coax the mare on.

Soon the horses felt soft long grasses stirring around their legs. The smell suffused the air. They knew they had arrived. That their long journey was ending. Abelinda gave a deep agonizing groan. It was discordant with the headiness of the moment.

"Bless my withers!" Corazón blurted. "Abelinda is foaling! A new foal is coming!"

Abelinda had lain down in a bed of the soft fragrant grass. Her eyes had rolled back in her head, and then they closed with relief as a little filly slipped out into the lingering light of the dawn.

"A new dawn horse!" Estrella whinnied. For a moment, her mind flashed back to the very beginning, before the beginning of their journey, to that time on the ship in the seconds after she was born and tried to stand. She had fallen of course. "Too many legs!" Her dam, Perlina, had laughed softly. "Well, little one, you'll have time to sort them out." The groom had quickly come and put her in a sling like the rest of the horses in the hold. None of the horses were allowed to stand free, for fear they would fall because of the ship's rollicking motion in the turbulent seas.

"Abelinda," Estrella said softly, "I was born on a ship. I never was allowed to stand. They put me in a sling. Imagine that!"

"No, I can't," said Abelinda. "For this one is born free." And at precisely that moment, a little mason bee swooped down and dropped some petals right on the foal's head.

"Grace!" Hope yipped. "You came! You came!"

"I told you that I would see you when the *Aurora salix* blooms. And these are the blossom of the dawn willow. The *Aurora salix.*"

"So you did."

The air now swirled with a small storm of petals. The horses gathered as close as they could to look at the little filly as she tried to stand on her wobbly legs.

"And what will you call her?"

"For the dawn, of course. This is the Valley of the Dawn. And so I shall name her Aurora, for the dawn. The same as you." Abelinda nodded toward the tiny horse, who now stood shoulder to shoulder with Estrella and dipped her head a bit. "And for short, we'll call her Rory."

"I am honored," the tiny horse whinnied. First Girl slipped onto the horse's back again.

The horse and the girl began to walk away. The herd watched them. The sparkling horse seemed not to fade but to become transparent, and within her, they began to see all the other horses that had come through time from that first horse. Each horse appeared to melt into another one with features more like their own, the ones of the first herd. The horse stopped, and First Girl turned around and looked directly into Tijo eyes as if to say, *And this is where you began.* Both Tijo and Estrella understood. It was as Tijo had told her once:

We are long spirits. Time weavers. We weave between the oceans of time like the shuttle of Haru's loom. We see the cloth of the future and that of the ancient past. We are both of us threads in the same blanket.

The sun rose. The foal stood. The herd grazed in this place of the sweet grass, where time had briefly stopped and so many threads had merged into this flow of life since the very beginning of a new world.

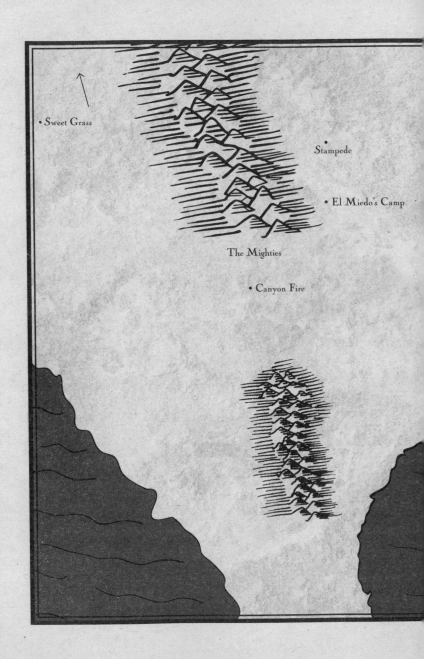

Sweet Grass

Stampede

El Miedo's Camp

The Mighties

Canyon Fire

N

First
Island

About the Author

Kathryn Lasky is the author of the bestselling Guardians of Ga'Hoole series, which has more than seven and a half million copies in print, as well as the Wolves of the Beyond series. Her books have received a Newbery Honor, a Boston Globe–Horn Book Award, and a Washington Post–Children's Book Guild Award. She lives with her husband in Cambridge, Massachusetts.

Out of the darkness, heroes will rise...

Also Available:

by Kathryn Huang

by Kathryn Huang & Kathryn Lasky

Read them all!

www.scholastic.com/gahoole

GAHOOLE15